My Cup Runneth Over

Other Books by Debbie Viguié

The Psalm 23 Mysteries

The Lord is My Shepherd
I Shall Not Want
Lie Down in Green Pastures
Beside Still Waters
Restoreth My Soul
In the Paths of Righteousness
For His Name's Sake
Walk Through the Valley
The Shadow of Death
I Will Fear No Evil
Thou Art With Me
Thy Rod and Thy Staff
Comfort Me
A Table Before Me
In the Presence of Mine Enemies
Anointest My Head With Oil

The Kiss Trilogy

Kiss of Night
Kiss of Death
Kiss of Revenge

Sweet Seasons

The Summer of Cotton Candy
The Fall of Candy Corn
The Winter of Candy Canes
The Spring of Candy Apples
The Summer of Rice Candy

A Salty Tale Mysteries

The Spice of Life
The Salt of the Earth (coming soon!)

My Cup Runneth Over

Psalm 23 Mysteries

By Debbie Viguié

Published by Big Pink Bow

My Cup Runneth Over

Copyright © 2019 by Debbie Viguié

ISBN-13: 978-1-7334281-2-5

Published by Big Pink Bow

www.bigpinkbow.com

All rights reserved.

Dedicated to Becky Lewis for her tireless encouragement and support. Thank you.

1

Detective Mark Walters had a love-hate relationship with Thursdays. On the one hand they were the harbinger of Fridays, which still meant something to him even if he did end up working more weekends than he would like. There was a weird sort of restless, impatient anticipation that came with the day. He personally liked that feeling. What he didn't like was when other people couldn't cope with that feeling. And, of course, being the day after a major holiday just made things crazier.

That's why he wasn't entirely surprised to be staring at a dead body. What *did* surprise him was that he'd been the one to stumble across it.

In his backyard.

Well, technically it wasn't *his* backyard. It was just the backyard of the house Traci and he were renting while they waited for insurance to finish up doing whatever it was they were doing regarding their old house which had burnt to the ground. Joseph and Geanie had been kind enough to invite them to stay with them indefinitely, but he had thought that in order to return to some semblance of normality they should find their own place. They had moved in a week earlier. Clearly, that had been a mistake.

"Go back inside, Buster," Mark told he dog, unclipping the leash from his collar.

Buster looked at him for a moment and then went in the house. Mark closed the sliding glass door behind him. The yard wasn't fenced so he'd been taking Buster for his morning constitutional. Buster had seen the body first, baying to let Mark know that there was trouble.

The body was that of a young woman. Mark judged her to be somewhere around twenty. She was splayed out on the lawn. She had bruises and a deep, red mark around her throat. If he had to guess, he'd say that her killer had just let the body fall after choking her to death.

He'd called it in immediately. Now, three minutes later, he found it difficult not to approach the body and start examining it and the scene more closely. He knew better, though. Officers needed to grab some pictures before anyone else got any closer. He was hoping they'd be able to find some footprints out there that weren't his or the victim's.

Even more upsetting than finding a dead body in his backyard was knowing that she had likely been killed there while he had been sleeping inside. He hadn't heard anything. It didn't make him feel much better, though. He wished he could have saved her.

He heard the sliding glass door open.

"Mark?" Traci called.

"Don't come out here," he said gruffly as he turned to face her.

"What's wrong?" she asked.

She'd been a cop's wife long enough to know what it meant when he used that tone of voice. She'd been his wife long enough to know when he was being evasive, so he decided not to bother. As soon as the first squad car got there it would be obvious anyway.

"There's a dead body on the lawn."

"Oh no!"

"I don't recognize her. It's a young woman," Mark said, to forestall the obvious next question. "It looks like someone murdered her."

Traci said something that was thoroughly unladylike yet highly appropriate.

"Put money in the swear jar," he said automatically.

She said something else worthy of the jar before closing the door.

Mark was still finding it weird that Traci had become a Christian. Logically, he saw how she got there. It just was taking some getting used to on his part. Mostly to cover up his own sense of anxiety he had started teasing her mercilessly on the rare occasions that she swore. He had created the jar and made her put money in it every time she said something he deemed worthy of it. He had joked that they'd take the money and use it for a vacation. So far they had enough for about a quarter of a tank of gas.

He recognized that it was childish on his part, but fortunately his wife understood him and his coping mechanisms well enough to go along with it. Now, if she came to the realization that she should start making him pay in, then he'd be in trouble. Of course, the presence of tiny, innocent ears in the house had already made him curtail his language far more than any swear jar could ever do.

He could hear cars arriving at the front of the house. He was grateful that they'd left off their sirens. The last thing they needed was to alert the whole neighborhood to their problem. At least, not at six in the morning.

If I'd been alerted last night that she had a problem, there'd be no need to worry about it now, he thought.

He could hear men walking next to the side of the house. He turned and saw two officers, Taylor and Monroe, round the corner of the house.

"Morning," Mark said.

Taylor held up his hand. "Sir, I'm going to ask you to step inside the house for a few minutes."

"Very funny," Mark said, not exactly in the mood for a joke.

"Sir, I-" Taylor turned fully toward him and stopped abruptly. "Detective Walters?"

"Last time I checked."

"What are you doing here in your robe?"

"I live here," Mark said, narrowing his eyes.

Monroe busted out laughing.

"Why didn't you tell me where we got called to?" Taylor asked the other officer.

"Because of this. The look on your face is priceless," Monroe said.

Mark heard more footsteps and a moment later Liam rounded the corner with a scowl on his face.

"Break it up, you two," he snapped. "Have some respect for the dead."

"Sorry, sir," Monroe said.

"Sorry," Taylor muttered.

Liam turned to Mark and gave him the tiniest of smiles.

This kind of work was emotionally taxing in a way most people could never understand. He didn't blame the other two for their jocularity. Heaven knew Mark had developed

4

a strong sense of gallows humor. He was sure he'd said some inappropriate things before, but he did his best to not appear flippant in front of witnesses.

"Maybe it would be a good idea for you to wait inside while the officers secure the crime scene," Liam said.

"Whatever you say," Mark said.

He turned and went into the house. Liam came with him. As soon as he had closed the sliding glass door, he looked at Mark and rolled his eyes.

"Sorry about Tweedledee and Tweedledum out there."

"Frankly I'm just glad Taylor no longer looks like he's going to vomit when he arrives at a crime scene."

Liam chuckled.

Mark sat down at the dining table and Liam did the same.

"How are you holding up?" Liam asked.

"As well as can be expected, I think."

"Tell me what happened."

"I got up, put on the coffee, turned on the backyard lights, grabbed my phone, and took Buster out for a walk."

"And what time was that?"

"Approximately 5:48."

"Okay, then what?"

"We only made it a few steps. Buster bayed like there was something wrong, something in the yard. That's when I saw the young woman."

"Where she is she should have been clearly visible due to the lights. How come you didn't see her right off?"

"Because I was staring straight ahead and up, not looking off to the left and on the ground where she is."

"Then what?"

"I called it in. Once I had I sent Buster back into the house. Traci opened the door a couple minutes later. I told her there was a dead body. She closed the door and I kept waiting until Tweedledee and Tweedledum showed up."

"Did you touch the body or anything else?"

"No."

Mark knew it was Liam's job to ask. He didn't begrudge him that. It wasn't unheard of for a law enforcement officer who knew better to touch a body or contaminate the crime scene when they were the ones who found the body at home or somewhere else unexpected. Shock had a way of short-circuiting the logic centers of the brain. Even he'd had to fight the urge to examine the body. Curiosity and the need to understand were two huge driving factors of human nature and they were still present even when logic was on vacation.

"Is it normal for you to carry your cell with you on these morning walks?"

"Yes. Buster often takes a couple of minutes and I check messages, email, weather, whatever."

"Did you recognize the young woman?"

"No."

"Did Traci?"

"Traci didn't see the body. I told her not to come outside."

"Did you hear any noises outside?"

"No. Nothing," Mark said, trying to keep his frustration under control.

"Did Buster bark last night?"

"No, he was asleep in the bedroom all night. There wasn't a peep from him. Then again, I'm convinced he couldn't hear a freight train going through here when he's really out. He snores very loudly."

"So does your wife," Liam commented.

"What?" Mark asked. "How do you know that?"

"You've told me. And, even if you hadn't, anyone who's been in the same wing when you stay at Joseph's has heard her."

"Yeah, it's pretty epic," Mark admitted.

"So, I think it's plausible that you didn't hear anything last night."

"Gee, thanks for giving me the benefit of the doubt. Makes me feel all warm and fuzzy."

Liam shrugged. "If a body dropped on any other lawn the first people you and I would be questioning would be the homeowners."

"I know, that's exactly what I've done, remember?" Mark said, thinking about the body of the homeless man that had turned up on Jeremiah's lawn.

Liam looked at him quizzically.

"Sorry, I forgot that was before your time," Mark muttered.

"Let me get this straight. You didn't see anything. You didn't hear anything. You don't know anything."

"That's right."

"Why do I feel like we're in New York?" Liam joked.

"Well, it happens to be true," Mark said. "I wish I had heard anything. Maybe if I had-"

"No," Liam said, cutting him off. He shook his head sternly. "Don't go there. There was no way you could have known. There was nothing you could have done to help. Understand?"

"Yes," Mark said, forcing himself to take a deep breath.

"Morning, Liam," Traci said as she came into the room. She had dressed and looked far more ready to tackle the day than Mark was.

"Morning, Traci. Sorry about all this."

Traci nodded.

"Thank you," she said. "Let me know when you're ready to question me."

"We can get that over with now while Mark goes and puts on some clothes," Liam suggested.

"Thank you," Mark said, standing up.

He beat a hasty retreat to the bedroom where he quickly changed clothes under Buster's watchful eye.

"It's unnerving when you stare at me like that," Mark told the dog.

Buster just blinked and rested his head down on the bed.

"Maybe the excitement of your day is over, but mine is just getting started," Mark told him.

Once he had gotten completely changed, he poked his head into the twins' bedroom to check on them. They were both still asleep which was a small mercy. He tiptoed back out of the room, hoping that he hadn't disturbed them. Sometimes he swore that they could tell when someone was looking at them and wake from a dead sleep in response.

As he crept back down the hallway all seemed well. He must have gotten away with it. Still, he breathed easier once he made it back to the dining room. Traci stood up from the table when she saw him.

"Please, don't let me interrupt," he said.

"She was done hours ago," Liam said with a smile.

"Would you like me to make some breakfast?" she asked, eyeing both of them.

8

Mark desperately wanted to say yes. Normally he just grabbed something like a yogurt or a bagel for breakfast. Still, he didn't want her to have to put forth the effort.

Liam smiled. "You know I'm not one to turn down home cooking, but please don't put yourself out on my account."

"It's fine," she said. "Hon, you want anything?"

"Yes!" Mark said eagerly.

Traci turned away but he saw her smile before she did so. She was handling the whole thing remarkably well. If their roles had been reversed he was fairly certain he would have been more of a wreck.

She started moving about the kitchen, gathering things to make pancakes. Mark's stomach grumbled noisily in anticipation. He turned back to Liam, trying to focus on the murder at hand.

In the kitchen Traci began humming softly. It struck him as odd. Liam looked puzzled as well.

Mark stood up and walked over to stand beside Traci.

"Honey, you feeling okay?" he asked.

"Yes," she said, smiling faintly.

"Are you sure?"

"I'm sure."

"Because you know we've got a dead body in the backyard."

"I know."

"Then why is it that you're smiling?" he asked, bewildered.

"Because I'm wondering how long it takes before one of you calls Jeremiah and asks if he left it there."

9

2

Jeremiah was in the middle of a dream when his phone rang and woke him up. He grabbed it and saw that Mark was calling.

"Hello?" he asked groggily.

"Did you kill anyone last night?" the detective asked bluntly.

"Not that I'm aware of," Jeremiah said with a yawn. "What's going on?"

"There's a dead body in my backyard."

"What?" Jeremiah asked as he sat up in alarm. "Are you okay?"

"We're fine, just a bit… confused, put out, I don't know what to call it."

"Why did you think I had something to do with it?"

"I didn't. Traci made a comment, though, and… look, I figured if it was you then you would have at least had the courtesy to call me and let me know before I found it this morning."

"Depends on the circumstances," Jeremiah said.

"Thanks, that's very reassuring," Mark said sarcastically.

"Sorry, if you wanted reassurance you should have called someone else."

"Clearly." Mark sighed audibly. "Still, everything okay with you?"

"Yeah."

"You at home?"

"Yes. Do you want me to come over?"

"No. It should be fine. I'll call if I need anything."

"Okay."

Mark hung up and Jeremiah sat for a moment staring at the phone. Next to him Captain yawned noisily and reached out to put a paw on Jeremiah's leg.

"I know, but what was he trying to say about Traci?" Jeremiah asked the German shepherd.

Mark had told him not to come over, but Jeremiah couldn't shake the feeling that he should. He got up, much to Captain's disgust. A minute later he was getting dressed. He decided to wear a long-sleeved button down light blue shirt that Cindy had given him for Christmas the day before. It was the first time that someone had given him an article of clothing as a gift since he was a kid. As he looked in the mirror he had to admit that it did look good on him, just as she had said it would.

After grabbing his wallet from the dresser he hesitated. He was debating whether or not to bring a weapon. He carried one most days anymore. However, he was heading over to an active crime scene crawling with police officers. Since it was at Mark's house, his friend would not be the one in charge of the crime scene either. He weighed the options. It wasn't like he had a permit for the gun he had been carrying. He also knew that the knife that was his preferred alternate weapon was illegal to carry in the state because of the length of the blade. Of course, he wore weapons all the time around police officers and the only one who'd ever caught him was Mark and it had been a

11

year since then. Plus, he never again intended to be caught without one when he needed it.

"This decision should not be so difficult," he told Captain.

He decided to leave the weapons at home, but he wasn't pleased about it. It seemed no one was having a good morning because Captain clearly wasn't pleased about being rousted out of bed for a quick morning walk. When they made it back into the house the dog ignored his food bowl in the kitchen and made straight for the bedroom. He was asleep again before Jeremiah could leave the house a minute later.

Not that he could blame Captain. The day before had been a big one, filled with lots of chaos and excitement. They had all celebrated Christmas at Geanie and Joseph's house. It was the first time he had fully participated in the festivities and it had felt very odd. The others shared a bond that he and Mark did not. The detective at least had more of a cultural connection, though. He could at least sing all the words to "Silent Night", which was apparently the most important Christmas song there was. At least that was the way it seemed. He wasn't sure what made that one any more special than the others, but it seemed to hit people on more of an emotional level somehow. For his money "O Come Emmanuel" was far more moving.

He shook his head. He doubted he'd ever truly get Christmas either in a religious sense or a cultural one. It just hadn't been a part of his upbringing at all. But it was important to Cindy so it was worth making an effort.

Captain had certainly been overjoyed with the mountain of presents he got, everything from new squeaky toys to a bed of his own for Cindy's house to a giant bone from the butcher's shop that still had some meat on it. That last had come from Liam and his girlfriend, Rebecca. Buster and Clarice had received ones as well.

The drive to the house that Mark and Traci were renting was a short one. It was in the same neighborhood as the house that Cindy used to rent from one of the church members. When he reached the house and saw the police cars out front he tensed up. He took a moment and reminded himself that as far as they were concerned he was an innocent man.

He was glad that he had followed the inner prompting to come over, even if he had to put on a smile and pretend like nothing was ever wrong. It couldn't be easy on Mark and Traci to be dealing with this fresh trauma at their new place. In truth what they probably needed more than anything else at the moment were his services as a counselor and a friend.

He found an out-of-the-way place to park. Then he approached the house slowly, hands kept well out to his sides. One of the officers saw and recognized him. Jeremiah just smiled and nodded at him.

Jeremiah reached the front door and after a moment's hesitation tried the doorknob. It was unlocked and he pushed the door open and stepped inside, closing it firmly behind him. He could hear voices coming from the dining room at the back of the house and he walked toward them.

"Hello, good morning," he called when he got close.

Traci popped her head out of the kitchen. She had what looked like flour on her pink shirt. "Hello, Jeremiah!" she said cheerfully.

A little too cheerfully, given the circumstances. It was more than that, though. Her voice had a sort of sing-song quality to it that was not normal for her.

"How are you doing?" he asked, struggling to hold onto his smile.

"Oh, you know, just another day at the Walters' residence, a beautiful day," she said.

Jeremiah felt his smile slipping. Before he could say anything he heard Mark call out.

"We're in the dining room!"

Jeremiah took a couple more steps until he could see into the entire kitchen and the dining room. Mark and Liam were seated at the dining room table. Liam had a notepad in front of him and was tapping it with a pen.

"Do you want some pancakes, Jeremiah?" Traci asked.

Her eyes were somewhat glassy looking. He realized that, even though he was hungry and would normally love some pancakes, there was no way he was eating anything she was preparing in the state she was in.

"No, I'm good, thank you."

He walked over to the dining table and chose a seat in the corner where he could easily watch the kitchen, dining room, and yard without turning his back on any of them.

He took a better look at the two men at the table. Mark looked a bit strained but mostly calm. Liam was concerned but was doing a good job of hiding it. They were both doing better than he could have asked for. Not like Traci.

Then again, neither of them were there when the last house blew up. Traci had been. That trauma was still fresh and he didn't like the look in her eyes now.

"Traci, why don't you come sit down for a minute?" he suggested.

She stopped and looked at him. "But I'm making pancakes."

"The pancakes can wait," Jeremiah said. "Come here for a minute, please."

Traci looked at the mixing bowl and then back at Jeremiah.

"Just real quick," he said gently.

"What-" Mark started to ask.

Jeremiah made a small sideward motion with his hand to indicate that Mark should stop talking. Fortunately, the detective saw and complied.

Traci walked slowly out of the kitchen. Her eyes were wide, her steps somewhat halting.

She reminded Jeremiah of a wild animal and he refrained from moving so as not to startle her. Mark and Liam also seemed to freeze and he was grateful for it.

Traci reached the chair next to his. She slowly sat down on it, keeping her eyes fixed on his face. Seeing her this close he realized just how bad off she was.

He breathed in slowly and she unconsciously mirrored him. He took several more slow, deep breaths and so did she. He slowly relaxed the corners of his mouth, letting his smile be smaller. She relaxed hers as well. She had been struggling to keep that smile on. He could tell.

She was in deep trouble, whether she realized it or not. He suspected that she had mentioned him to Mark for a reason. Her subconscious had been looking for some way, *any* way, to cope with what had happened.

He relaxed his face all the way until it was a neutral expression. He was neither smiling nor frowning. She did the same. He took a couple more deep breaths and so did she.

15

The glassiness of her eyes was changing. It was like watching someone wake up from a deep sleep. The muscles in her face began to twitch slightly, one at a time.

"Traci, I want you to listen to me very, very carefully," he said. "Can you do that?" he asked.

She nodded slowly and he nodded in time with her.

"Good, that's good. You're doing very good."

He reached out and placed his left hand very gently on top of her right hand where it rested on the table. The skin on her hand was cold to the touch. He repeated the action with his right hand, using it to cover her left.

"You're doing great. You believe me, right?"

Again she nodded and he did, too.

He could feel the unspoken questions from Mark and Liam, but both men stayed blessedly silent, not really moving, doing nothing to distract her. That was a very good thing under the circumstances.

He slowly moved his hands underneath hers. He folded her hands in his, holding them, warming them. She continued to stare at him. The muscles in her face were starting to twitch harder and more rapidly. She began to blink randomly, uncontrollably.

"You know that I want what's best for you and that I will tell you the truth," he said.

She nodded.

He took another deep breath and so did she.

He squeezed her hands in his, making sure she'd be able to feel the pressure.

"Traci, I promise you, everything is going to be alright."

She stared deep into his eyes and he nodded.

"It's going to be alright," he said, repeating himself. "You're going to be alright."

Her whole body began to shake, and a high-pitched wail escaped her lips. Reality was crashing in on her. She'd been in shock and a state of almost manic denial about what was happening. Now it was hitting her hard. On the heels of what had happened just a few weeks before it was too much and it was threatening to overwhelm her.

She tried to jerk her hands away as sobs wracked her body. Mark and Liam both started up from the table, but Jeremiah pulled her into his arms before they could do anything else.

She struggled against him for a moment, but he held her tight.

"I know," he said. "You know I know. I was there. I've seen the terrible things that happened. And I promise you, Traci, that it will be alright. You won't have to spend the rest of your life in fear."

She slumped and then a moment later buried her face in his chest and cried.

Mark and Liam both looked stricken. Each of them had been focused on dealing with the murder, figuring out what had happened, and getting the whole process taken care of as quickly as possible. Neither of them had realized that Traci was collapsing in on herself, fear and grief trying to overwhelm her to the point where her mind fought back the only way it knew how to. She had gone into denial, not dealing with the reality of what was happening.

He had seen this before. Her losses had been too devastating and too close together. He knew why Mark had been anxious for the family to get back into a place of their own, but they had done so too quickly. She felt safe at Geanie and Joseph's, and it was remarkable that she could feel safe anywhere. Mark didn't have the same issues because he hadn't been there. He hadn't been present when her entire world changed in one violent moment. The explosion had taken more from her than just her home. It had taken her sense of safety and security. Once lost those took a long time to recover, if ever.

Mark suddenly stepped forward, reaching out. Before Jeremiah could say something to stop Mark, the detective had put a hand on his wife's shoulder. She twisted, startled at feeling someone else touching her. Jeremiah made a clucking sound, trying to calm her down before she hurt Mark or herself.

"Traci, are you okay?" Mark asked, voice shaking.

"No!" she screamed at the top of her lungs.

3

Cindy was the first one up. She and Blackie had stayed overnight at Geanie and Joseph's house. She hadn't wanted Christmas to end and the four of them had stayed up late. Cindy, Geanie, and Joseph had talked far into the night while Blackie had pounced time and time again on Clarice who had passed out under the Christmas tree early on. The poodle had shown remarkable restraint. Either that or she was just too partied out to care.

Cindy was in the kitchen munching on some cinnamon holiday puffs that Geanie had made the day before. Her phone chimed, letting her know she had a text message. She picked it up and saw that it was from Kyle.

Headed to the airport.

What time do you land? she texted back.

Kyle and a camera crew were going to be at The Zone filming for the next few days.

5:15.

Then what?

Headed to hotel.

And? she asked.

That's it. No work til tomorrow.

Cindy took a deep breath. Things with Kyle had been considerably improved in the last few months.

Want to have dinner?

Love to! he texted.

Pick u up at 6:30?
Perfect!
:)
I'll treat you both.
It will just be you and me, she replied.
Y?
Bonding time for us.
K.
You'll see Jeremiah later I'm sure.
That's cool.

She hesitated a moment. She wanted to ask about their parents, but that was probably better done face-to-face.

Have a safe flight.
TY! <3 U.
<3 u 2.

She set her phone down on the counter and went back to eating. She honestly had mixed feelings about seeing Kyle. Things were a lot better between them which was nice. Still, she kept feeling like she was waiting for the other shoe to drop. She wasn't sure what it was going to take before she stopped feeling that way, but it was what it was.

She knew Jeremiah was having the same issue. That was part of the reason she had decided to just have her dinner with Kyle alone. It would give them a chance to be alone to talk and sort things out without having to worry about how anyone else was doing or feeling.

Things had come a long way since the days when she used his picture as a dart board. Still, there was more to do to solidify the relationship and build trust.

"Good morning," Geanie said as she came into the room.

"Morning."

"I see you're into the puffs," Geanie said. "That actually sounds like a good idea."

She put a couple of puffs on a plate and popped it into the microwave. She grabbed herself some orange juice and a minute later was sitting down next to Cindy with her food.

"I think I'm having déjà vu," Geanie admitted. "Just us having breakfast together like when we were roommates."

"Sometimes it feels like we still are," Cindy admitted.

Geanie chuckled. "It's nice to have this place filled with laughter and people."

"Once you guys have kids this place will be constantly filled with laughter."

"Maybe," Geanie muttered before biting into one of the puffs.

"You know, I really am glad that I gave Joseph my great-aunt's recipe for these things. He is such an amazing cook and I believe that he makes them even better than she used to. I just wish I knew how," Geanie said after finishing her bite.

There was one thing none of them had discussed over the last couple of weeks, at least, not that Cindy was aware of. Now New Year's Eve was less than a week away and there was literally an axe hanging over Geanie's head.

"We need to figure out what the plan is for New Year's Eve," Cindy said.

"You mean party?"

"No, the whole, secret society wants Joseph to kill you thing."

"Oh, that," Geanie said, making a face. "I know the guys have been discussing it."

"They have?" Cindy asked in surprise.

"So I've heard."

"Why haven't the girls been discussing it?"

"Because I don't want to," Geanie said. She picked up her second holiday puff and took a bite out of it.

"Why not? If it was me-"

"But it's not you," Geanie interrupted, speaking around the mouthful of puff.

Cindy paused and took a good look at her friend. Geanie looked subdued, sort of down. If Cindy really thought about it Geanie had looked that way for a while.

"Geanie, is there something wrong, something you're not telling me?"

Geanie looked at her and Cindy couldn't tell if she was on the verge of saying something or not. Suddenly the doorbell rang.

Geanie rolled her eyes. "If it's carolers, they're late."

"I'll get it," Cindy said.

She got up and headed for the front door. It was still pretty early and she wondered who it could be. She went to the front door and opened it.

Traci was standing on the porch with Buster at her side.

"Hi!" Cindy said, surprised to see her. "How are you?"

Traci launched herself forward. She hugged Cindy tight and began crying uncontrollably. Buster scampered past into the house barking to alert Clarice that he was there.

"What on earth?" Cindy asked.

Then through her sobs Traci managed to get out three words that chilled Cindy to the bone.

"It's never safe."

Cindy looked past Traci but could see no one else outside. Still holding on to the other woman she managed to shut and lock the door.

"Come with me," Cindy said, half-leading, half-dragging Traci to the kitchen.

"What's wrong?" Geanie asked, standing up when she saw them.

"I don't know."

"Where is everyone else?"

"She was alone."

"That can't be good," Geanie said, looking even more alarmed. "Let's get her into the sitting room."

Together Cindy and Geanie got Traci into the other room and all three of them sat down on one of the couches. Traci kept sobbing erratically.

"Traci, where are Rachel and Ryan?" Cindy asked.

"Jeremiah's taking them to Amber's house," the distraught woman barely managed to get out.

"Your sister Amber?" Cindy asked.

Traci nodded.

"Why?" Geanie asked sharply.

"Nothing bad ever happens there," Traci said.

When the four of them and Buster had left the night before they'd seemed in good spirits. Cindy couldn't help but worry about whatever had caused the change.

"Traci, where is Mark?" she asked, her stomach clenching as she waited for the answer.

"He's at the house with the body."

"What body?" Geanie asked.

"I don't know."

"Traci, sweetie, you're not making sense," Cindy said gently.

"He found a dead body in the backyard this morning," Traci finally managed to say after several seconds had passed.

It took all of Cindy's willpower to keep her voice calm and steady. "Was it anyone you knew?"

Traci shook her head. "It was a girl. We don't know who she is."

"It's going to be okay," Geanie said as she rubbed Traci's back.

"The only thing we know is that Jeremiah didn't kill her," Traci said.

"That's good," Cindy said, not sure how else to respond. It seemed like an odd thing for Traci to say.

"Why did God let this happen?" Traci asked.

"That's always the big question," Cindy said softly.

"God doesn't stop every bad thing that happens to us, but He does hold our hand and walk with us through them," Geanie answered.

"How do you know?" Traci asked as she stared at Geanie. "Bad things never happen to you."

Geanie bit her lip and looked quickly away. Cindy could see her shoulders bunch up with tension.

"Bad things have happened to her," Cindy said quickly. "Bad things have happened to both of us. Having God to turn to does help."

Traci dropped her head down and began to cry again.

~

Mark was scared. Traci was his rock and seeing her lose it like that had him more than a little freaked out. In the end he hadn't known what else to do but send her to Joseph and Geanie's house. It had been Jeremiah's suggestion to send the twins to stay with Traci's sister and brother-in-law for a couple of days. Mark didn't like it, but it made sense. It freed him up to focus on Traci.

That was something he desperately wanted to do, but first he had to wait until all the other police finished at his house. He was deeply grateful that Liam was taking point. He trusted his partner, but at the same time, he wasn't leaving their things unattended with other police around.

It wasn't that he had anything to hide. Well, not anything tangible at any rate. He had plenty of intangible things to hide that no amount of snooping through his stuff would reveal. He just didn't like the feeling of his privacy being invaded. He had a renewed sense of sympathy for those victims who had to have their houses searched.

What he had been able to glean so far was that the girl had no identification on her of any kind. That was strange. Stranger still was that she had no cell phone. She was wearing jeans and a pink and white striped shirt. While it appeared that she might have been choked to death with a wire or something similar, it was going to be up to the coroner to officially determine cause of death.

Officers were walking the neighborhood, asking Mark's new neighbors if they had seen or heard anything or if a young woman lived there who hadn't come home the night before. It was a logical assumption that she was from the neighborhood, though what she'd been doing in Mark's backyard was anyone's guess. It was possible she'd been running from someone who finally caught her.

His phone rang and he quickly answered.

"Hello?"

"It's Jeremiah. I've dropped Rachel and Ryan off. Where do you want me to go, your house or Geanie and Joseph's?"

"I think they're getting close to finishing here, so go to Geanie and Joseph's," Mark said. "I'll be heading there myself as soon as things are wrapped up."

Mark hung up and stared glumly at the backyard where the body had just been removed. Yellow police tape cordoned off his backyard, acting like the fence he didn't have. Once again his home was a crime scene. He didn't blame Traci for flipping out. It was getting on his nerves, too.

Liam came inside. He gave him a sympathetic look.

"I hate living in an active crime scene," Mark said.

"I know the feeling," Liam said. "It's never fun. You did the right thing to get the kids out of here. I know they're still really young, but it's funny how memories work. I remember things that happened when I was a little over a year old."

"Like what?" Mark asked.

"Things," Liam said with a shrug. "The good news is that everyone's clearing out. There wasn't much in the way of physical evidence outside. No clear footprints or anything useful like that."

"Still no word on who she was?"

"No. And, big surprise, nobody saw or heard anything." Mark sighed.

"You going to go pack a bag?" Liam asked.

"No need."

"You're staying?" Liam asked in surprise.

"No. I never unpacked last night."

~

Cindy felt a little bad leaving everyone that evening. Still there was nothing that could be done for Traci and Mark that wasn't already being done by other people. She had promised Kyle and the distraction would probably do her good.

He and the film crew were staying at The World Hotel that was next to The Zone theme park. As she entered the hotel lobby she had an unpleasant flashback to when she'd been sequestered there as a juror. The trial of Jason Todd had ended as a mistrial. She thought she'd heard something recently about a new trial that was about to take place. Hopefully this time justice would be served.

She tried to put it all from her mind. Tonight she needed more fun and less stress. She called Kyle's phone, but it went straight to voicemail. She marched up to the front desk and one of the staff looked up and smiled at her.

"May I help you, ma'am?" he asked.

"Yes, my brother, Kyle Preston, is staying here. Would you please ring his room for me?" she asked.

The man's eyes grew wide as he stared at something behind Cindy. She started to turn to see what he was looking at. Before she could, something grabbed her.

4

Cindy spun around with a scream.

Kyle was standing there, looking shocked.

"Oh no! I'm so sorry! I didn't mean to scare you," he said.

"Sorry, no, it's not you. It's me. It's been a weird day," she said. Although, truthfully, she probably would have screamed even if it hadn't been.

Kyle hugged her and she hugged him back.

"Sorry you've been having a day," he said.

"It's okay."

She let go of him and he stepped back, still looking a little sheepish. It was an odd look on him.

"Where do you want to eat dinner?" she asked.

"I figured I'd leave that up to my lovely dining companion," he said.

"How hungry are you?"

"Famished. I haven't eaten since early this morning."

"Okay, I'm thinking Rigatoni's."

"Italian?"

"Yes."

"Lead the way."

A minute later they were in the car and on their way.

"How was your Christmas?" Cindy asked.

"We missed you. Otherwise it was okay. Dad sends his love."

The omission of their mother was obvious. Cindy was fairly certain that it was just Kyle and their dad who had missed her.

"What did you do for Christmas?" he asked.

"A bunch of us spent it at Geanie and Joseph's," she said.

Kyle whistled. "I have to imagine they throw quite the shindig."

"Yes, they do."

"Were there live reindeer?"

"No!" Cindy said with a laugh. "It's a house, not a zoo."

"Trust me, I've been in houses. That is not a house. That's a palace."

"And it reigns over what, the kingdom of Coulter?"

"Works for me. Although Coulterland sounds better."

"It does," she admitted. "The decorations are still up. I'm sure we could find time this week for you to see them."

"I'm not sure everyone wants to see me," he said quietly.

She glanced at him. "No one blames you for what happened."

"I blame me," he said.

"Well stop. No one is to blame for Mom except Mom. You couldn't have kept her from going crazy."

"Neither could you."

"That's right."

"Sorry, on to happier subjects," he said.

"I'm all for that. So, what is it you're filming at The Zone?" Cindy asked.

"We're actually filming a couple of specials and segments for a couple of other shows. The big one is a New

Year's Eve party that's going to air live on New Year's Eve."

"Wow! Like a ball drop party?"

"Yup. We'll have some pre-recorded segments for the live show, but most of it will be live. Then we're doing a segment for our roller coaster special and a few other things."

"Wow, that's ambitious."

"Well, Flint Stevenson, the owner of the Escape! Channel loves to save money and kill as many birds with one stone as he can."

"Have you ever hosted a live event before?"

"No," he said. "I have participated in a few."

"That's right. You were in the Rose Parade one year," she said.

"Yes, I was. This is my first time actually hosting, being in charge of something like this."

"That must be exciting," she said.

He laughed. "Actually, it's nerve wracking."

"Seriously?" she asked, somewhat surprised. "All the crazy things you do and hosting a show is what freaks you out?"

"Yeah, there are no second takes, no do-overs. If something goes wrong it's out there for all the world to see with no way to take it back," he said.

"What's the worst that could happen?"

"I lose my career."

He was genuinely anxious about it. Her brother and she had made great strides in the last couple of years to try and understand each other and have a better relationship. Still, there was a perverse part of her that deep down was enjoying his anxiety. It must have somehow showed on her face.

"You think this is funny, don't you?" he asked.

"No," she said, struggling to keep a straight face.

"You're lying. You're about to start laughing any second. I tell you that I'm deathly afraid of flubbing my lines or having a wardrobe malfunction or something and all you can do is laugh."

"It is pretty funny," she admitted after a giggle escaped her.

"Well, at least now I know who not to come to when I need sympathy."

His tone and the expression on his face were not nearly as harsh as his words. In fact, she could swear she caught him smiling.

"That is true. It's good you've figured this out ahead of time," Cindy said.

"Do you do this to everyone? Laugh at their misfortune?"

"Stress laughter is a defense. And I only do it if I know for sure everyone is okay."

"I used to be that way," he said.

"What happened to change it?"

"I stopped laughing altogether."

"I've seen you laugh," she said.

"Not often and most of the time I'm faking it," he said.

"I'm sorry," she said as an unexpected wave of sorrow washed over her. "That's a terrible way to live."

"Thanks," he said, giving her a pained smile.

~

Jeremiah stayed and had dinner with the others before excusing himself and heading home. It had been a rough day and he was looking forward to some quality downtime with Captain.

When he turned onto his street, he was surprised to find another car in his driveway and the lights on in his house. He sat there for a moment, staring and thinking. Someone had broken into his house and clearly wasn't making an effort to be subtle about it. The only person besides Cindy and himself who ever had a reason to be at his house was Marie. Sometimes she looked after the house or Captain for him. There was no reason for her to be there at the moment, though. Plus, it wasn't her car out front.

He debated his options, running a number of scenarios through his mind. He finally settled on the simplest one. He got out of the car and walked up to the front door. It was unlocked. He managed to silently open it just a crack and then listened. From inside he could hear a muffled male voice.

Jeremiah opened the door and slipped inside, shutting it silently behind him. The voice was clearer now, coming from the living room.

"You just don't get enough attention, do you?" a man was saying in a tone of voice people usually reserved for children.

Jeremiah walked into the living room and found Martin there, roughhousing with Captain.

"It's bad enough when you invade my life. Must you also invade my house?" Jeremiah asked the C.I.A. operative.

"I wouldn't have to if you kept your phone charged," Martin said, not bothering to look up from staring into

Captain's eyes. "Your daddy shouldn't be so careless," he told the dog.

Jeremiah took his phone out of his pocket and noticed that it was indeed dead. He put it on the charger and returned to scrutinize Martin.

"What do you want, Martin?" he asked.

"Aside from quality time with a very good dog?" Martin asked, still vigorously petting Captain who was clearly enjoying it.

"Yes."

"Nothing."

Jeremiah rolled his eyes. "You didn't come here because there's nothing you want."

Martin looked up at him. "This is more of a courtesy call. I wanted to let you know that I'm in your neck of the woods for the next week."

"More terrorists?" Jeremiah asked.

Martin laughed. "Not the kind you're thinking of. I'm here on vacation."

Jeremiah frowned. "Why here?"

"The Zone and assorted other attractions in the southern California area. I might not have bothered to say anything, but I see your future brother-in-law is in town filming at The Zone. What were the odds?"

"Good question."

"I figure you and yours will be hanging around there more than usual. I didn't want any surprises. I like to keep my work life and my personal life as separate as possible."

"I can understand that."

Martin gave Captain a last scratch on the head before standing up.

"I walked him about half an hour ago," he said.

"Did you feed him, too?" Jeremiah asked.

"I do not recall," Martin said with a smirk.

"Have a good vacation," Jeremiah said.

"Thank you."

Martin left and Jeremiah looked at Captain and shook his head.

"You realize you're supposed to keep strangers *out* of the house, right?"

Captain tilted his head to the side, his tongue hanging out of his mouth. He turned and looked toward the front door and whined softly.

Jeremiah sat down on the couch and petted him on the head. "Do you believe he's here on vacation?"

Captain gave him a quizzical look.

"Yeah, I'm not sure what to think either," Jeremiah said.

~

Mark had gotten Traci to sleep. Once he had he'd gone downstairs and he was in the kitchen making himself a snack when Joseph appeared.

"I thought you guys turned in early," Mark said.

"Trouble sleeping," Joseph said with a grimace.

"I hear that. Can I get you anything? We've got sandwich makings and all kinds of different snacks. I could make you some tea. We've got some of that stuff that's supposed to help you sleep."

Mark realized after he'd said it that it made it sound like it was his kitchen and Joseph was the guest.

"Sleeping tea would be great," Joseph said.

"I'll make some for both of us."

As soon as the tea was ready Mark sat down next to Joseph and they both began to sip the tea.

"So, where are we on the whole killing my wife on New Year's Eve thing?" Joseph asked.

"Police protective custody," Mark said.

"You're joking."

"I haven't been able to find out anything else about this group and frankly I'm running out of options."

Joseph shook his head. "I'd hire a private army to protect Geanie if it came down to that."

"Why bother? With Jeremiah around who really needs an army?" Mark asked darkly.

"Only one problem with that," Joseph said. "He can't be everywhere, and he can't stay in one place all of the time. One of these days he's going to be five minutes too late."

"Please don't say that," Mark said, shuddering at the thought. That reality was just too horrible to imagine. It really was crazy how much he'd come to rely on his friend's darker skills, the very ones he'd once found suspect.

I was right to suspect him. I'm even more right to trust him.

"Aside from that issue, how is everything going?" Mark asked. It seemed like a ridiculous question, especially since they'd just spent the last couple of days together.

"Not as well as I'd like," Joseph admitted.

"Geanie still not pregnant?"

"No, and, frankly, I'm worried."

"Don't worry. These things can just take some time."

"That's not it. I'm worried that there's something wrong with her."

"Like what?" Mark asked.

"I don't know. I keep getting this nagging feeling in the back of my mind that there's some health issue we don't know about."

Mark had been hoping to get away from doom and gloom conversation for a little while, but apparently there was no escaping it.

At least not tonight.

He took a sip of his tea while he thought about what Joseph had just said.

"Have you been to a doctor?" he asked.

"Yes, but I'm thinking it's time to call in a specialist."

"On the plus side, at least you can afford the best in the country."

Joseph grunted and drank half his cup of tea.

"What about you?" Joseph asked after setting his cup down.

"You mean, other than today?"

"Yeah."

"Traci wants us to start going to church."

"How do you feel about that?"

"Less than thrilled."

"How much less?"

"Considerably," Mark admitted.

"One of these days you're going to have to come to terms with the fact that you're not an atheist, you know."

"I know. I was just hoping to do that in thirty or forty years," Mark said. He knew he was in a bit of a messed up place once the words left his mouth. He couldn't believe he had actually just admitted that.

"What are you scared of?" Joseph asked.

"Having to sit around drinking tea having conversations with people saying 'isn't God so great' when he's not."

36

"This right here is what you find so scary?" Joseph asked, hoisting his cup of tea.

"Not you specifically. Although if you'd told me a few years ago that you and I were going to be close friends, I wouldn't have believed it."

"Why?"

"Because you're such a churchy kind of guy, you know. I bet you've never had one negative thought about God in your whole life."

Joseph chuckled. "There was a time when I thought God was quite a jerk. I told Him so. Repeatedly. Using much more colorful language, I might add."

"You? I don't believe it," Mark said dismissively.

"Oh yeah. For about a year the only time I talked to Him was when I wanted to scream at Him."

"What went so wrong in your perfect little world that you acted out like that?" Mark didn't mean to be sarcastic, but it slipped out anyway.

"My parents died when I was fourteen. My legal guardian was unfit to look after a goldfish and I had to fight to be emancipated."

"I had no idea," Mark said, stunned by the revelation.

"Why? Because I'm such a nice, normal guy?" Joseph asked in a sarcastic tone.

"Um normal, no, but nice, yes and level-headed."

"Thanks."

"So, what made you stop yelling at God?"

"More of a 'who' than a 'what'."

"Okay, who?"

"A dog and a bum."

Before Mark could say anything he heard the front door open.

~

Cindy walked into the kitchen to find Mark and Joseph sitting at the counter. Both men looked tired.

"Hey, everything okay?" she asked.

"Fine. How was dinner with Kyle?" Joseph asked.

"Good, actually. Are you expecting company tonight?"

"Not this late, why?" Joseph asked with a frown.

"I think a car turned up the hill after I did. I didn't see them when I parked, though."

The doorbell rang.

"That must be whoever," Cindy said. "I can get it."

Both men nodded at her, clearly grateful not to have to stand up.

Cindy returned to the entryway and hesitated for a moment. What could someone possibly want here at this hour? She wondered if maybe she should have Mark answer the door instead. She decided she was just being jumpy.

She resolutely opened the door. A young woman was standing on the porch looking very unsure. She had her arms wrapped around herself. There was something about her that was familiar, but Cindy couldn't put her finger on where she'd seen her before.

"Can I help you?" Cindy asked cautiously.

"I'm here to see my sister, Traci."

All of a sudden Cindy knew who it was. The last time she had seen her she had been unconscious and an F.B.I. agent was taking her into protective custody.

"Lizzie!"

5

Cindy opened the door wide and stepped aside to let Lizzie in. She closed and locked the door and then led Lizzie into the kitchen.

"Lizzie! What are you doing here?" Mark asked as he stood up.

"I was at Amber's when Jeremiah brought the twins over. I heard what happened. You were there for me when I needed you. I was hoping to return the favor," Lizzie said. "I didn't mean to get here so late, but there was an accident on the freeway and I was stuck for a while."

Mark gave Lizzie a smile.

"Traci will be glad you're here," he said.

Lizzie looked good. She had put on a little weight and her hair was now a dark blond color. All-in-all she looked almost nothing like she had when Cindy had met her two Halloweens before.

Lizzie looked nervous and uncomfortable.

"Where is my sister?" she asked.

"I got her to sleep," Mark said.

Joseph stood up and held out his hand. "Hello, I'm Joseph. Not sure you'd remember me."

"Hi," Lizzie said, timidly shaking his hand.

"Can Mark make you anything, a sandwich, some tea? He's running the kitchen tonight."

"I could use some tea," Cindy said.

Lizzie shook her head and yawned.

"You look tired. Did you bring a bag with you?" Joseph asked.

"Yes. If Traci's asleep I guess I should go find a hotel."

"Nothing doing," Mark said. "We have plenty of room here."

Joseph looked like he was trying really hard not to laugh.

"Joseph, which room should we put her in?" Mark asked.

"I'm sure whatever room you think will be fine," Joseph said with a smirk.

"There's one just down the hall from us that will be great," Mark said. "Let's get your bag from the car and I'll show you."

Lizzie nodded. Mark led her toward the foyer and as soon as they were outside, Joseph let out the laughter he'd been holding in.

"What was that?" Cindy asked.

"Apparently Mark's starting to feel really at home here," Joseph said.

A couple of minutes later Mark returned and poured himself another cup of tea. He sat down with a weary sigh.

"You okay?" Cindy asked.

"We need a vacation," Mark said.

"We all do," Joseph said.

"Hah! Can you imagine us all going on vacation together? It would be like inviting disaster," Mark said.

"Well, at least we would know it's coming if we invited it. Usually it just crashes the party."

"The last time I went on vacation my brother and the rest of us were nearly killed," Cindy said.

"Geanie and I missed that one," Joseph said.

"Trust me, you didn't miss anything," Mark said.

"And the time before that I got kidnapped and nearly killed," Cindy said.

"Our last vacation was great except for the homicide we had to help solve," Mark said.

"Our last vacation was our honeymoon and it was great," Joseph said.

"Then that's what we've been doing wrong. We all need to go on vacation with you," Mark said.

"I've got a dog show in Florida at the end of February. You're all welcome to join us," Joseph said.

~

The next morning at breakfast Traci seemed to be doing much better, which was a relief to Cindy. The other woman was clearly also happy that her sister had driven out to spend time with her. Lizzie looked a little more relaxed than she had the night before.

Joseph made a gourmet breakfast which Mark tried to claim the credit for. It felt like a normal, crazy morning at the Coulter house. However, she wished Jeremiah was there with them. At least she had talked to him that morning and he'd let her know he couldn't join them all until evening. He had work to do at the synagogue.

They had just finished eating when Geanie rose dramatically from her chair. All eyes swiveled toward her.

"I have declared Girls' Day," Geanie announced.

"What does that mean?" Mark asked.

"It means we don't get to play, or we're off the hook, depending on how you look at it," Joseph said.

"What are we going to do?" Cindy asked.

"We're going to go play at The Zone. Then we can watch Kyle do some filming *if* we want to," Geanie said.

"Sounds good to me," Traci said.

"Who is Kyle?" Lizzie asked.

"Cindy's brother," Geanie said.

"Kyle Preston. He's an Escape! Channel star," Traci said.

"Kyle Preston is your brother?" Lizzie asked, turning to gawk at Cindy.

Cindy nodded.

"That guy's crazy!" Lizzie blurted out.

"It has been said," Cindy told her.

"And not just by Cindy," Geanie said.

"Does Amber know?" Lizzie asked.

"Oh yeah," Traci said, looking smug. "But she hasn't met him, so you'll be one up on her."

"Yes!" Lizzie said excitedly.

Cindy couldn't help but smile. Traci's older sister loved to brag about celebrities she'd spotted in public, particularly Chuck Norris.

"So, it's decided. Let's meet back here in ten minutes with shoes on," Geanie said. She then hurried out of the room.

"Shoes on?" Lizzie asked in a puzzled voice. She glanced down at the shoes she was already wearing.

"It means ready to walk out the door," Joseph translated.

"Let's go," Traci said, grabbing Lizzie's hand and pulling her toward the doorway.

Cindy lingered for a moment, staring at Mark and Joseph.

"Are you guys going to be okay?" she asked them.

"I'm going into the precinct to see what they've found out about the dead girl in our backyard," Mark said.

"And I have work to do," Joseph said.

"You actually do work?" Mark asked.

Joseph rolled his eyes. "Just because you don't see it doesn't mean it doesn't happen."

~

Mark was relieved that Traci was looking better than she had the day before. He headed down to the precinct, hoping that there would be something on the mystery body from the backyard. The sooner they could get this solved and move on the better for everyone.

He was glad the ladies were going to be spending the day in the park. He wouldn't have to worry about them as much. With any luck he could join them later in the day.

He was still driving a rental car. Insurance hadn't finished sorting out the entire firebombing mess that had taken out his car. He was past ready to get his life back to some semblance of normal.

Once inside the precinct he took off his jacket and sat down at his desk. Before he could even check his desk for messages Wendell, the department's sole remaining computer guru, walked up and dropped some papers on the desk. Mark looked up at him.

"What are these?" Mark asked.

Wendell rolled his eyes. "Remember you asked me to follow the money and find whoever was paying for the old lady you killed in that rest home?"

"How could I forget?" Mark said with a sigh.

"That's what I was wondering."

"And she attacked me."

"Yup. You've got to watch out for little old ladies like that. Dangerous."

"You weren't there," Mark said, anger racing through him.

"Not until afterward."

"What took you so long to run this down?" Mark asked, tapping the papers.

"Half the department was a little bit busy trying to hunt down the mistletoe killer."

Mark nodded. Jackson had been the lead detective on that but everyone in the precinct had heard about it. Two couples on opposite ends of town had been murdered and their bodies left in such a way that it looked like they were kissing under mistletoe. Mark had been grateful that for once he hadn't gotten one of the bizarre cases. Plus, he'd been busy with other things.

"You catch the guy?" Mark asked.

"Not yet," Wendell said with a scowl.

That wasn't a good sign, especially given that the Christmas season had just ended. The national clearance rate for murders was only slightly higher than 60%. While their department had a higher solve rate, there was still a decent chance that the killer would never be caught.

Like Matthews.

Not Paul's dad was still managing to cause trouble decades after he'd killed or aided in the suicide of his cult and left the area. At least, he was causing trouble for Mark. He couldn't let it go. Part of him really wanted to, but with every new thing that happened it became harder to do.

"So, did you find the one paying the bills for the old lady?"

"You're not going to even pretend to read the report?" Wendell asked sarcastically.

"Not at the moment."

"Fine. I'll spare you the effort. It's a dead end."

"A dead end?"

"That's what I said."

"How is that possible?"

"Shell companies, overseas accounts, it's all in the report if you want the details. The bottom line is we don't know who was paying for her to be there."

Mark closed his eyes as he felt a headache coming on. That was definitely not what he wanted to hear.

"So, unless you have something else for me, there's nothing more I can do for you on that."

"Thanks for trying," Mark said. He was being sincere.

"You're, uh, welcome," Wendell said, clearly thrown off.

Wendell turned abruptly and left.

"What was that about?" Liam asked as he walked up.

"Got a big, fat nothing as to who was paying the bills at the rest home."

"I'm sorry," Liam said.

"It's not your fault."

"Yeah, but you haven't been having a great day."

"Any chance it's going to get better?" Mark asked.

Liam shook his head.

"Do we at least know who the victim was?"

"Brie Vargas, eighteen. Lived two blocks away."

"How did she end up in my backyard?"

"Don't know that yet, but it was confirmed that she was killed there."

"Great," Mark said. "Nothing makes a house a home like a murder in the backyard."

"It could be worse."

"How?"

"You could be the owners of the house instead of renters."

"Imagine my relief at this moment," Mark said, not bothering to try and hide the sarcasm in his voice.

~

"So, where shall we start?" Geanie asked after they'd made it into The Zone.

"The Atomic Coaster," Traci said. "I want to do that before lunch."

"That's in the Exploration Zone," Geanie said, leading the way.

"Why before lunch?" Lizzie asked.

"Because otherwise I'll throw up," Traci said.

"We all might," Geanie added.

A couple minutes later they were standing in front of an imposing metal structure that reached to the sky. The atomic coaster was meant to resemble a giant atom. It had four tracks that were oval in shape. One vertical and two diagonal ones moved around the nucleus in the center. The horizontal track was where the cars loaded and unloaded.

"We're going on that?" Lizzie asked.

"Yup," Traci said.

"Cindy!" someone called out.

Cindy turned and saw a cotton candy cart a few feet away. Its operator was waving excitedly at her. She recognized her as Brenda, one of the high school girls who went to the church. Cindy had driven her and some of the others one Thanksgiving as they gave out meals to needy families in the community. Unfortunately, no one had realized in time that they were sending Brenda to visit her own family.

Cindy walked up to the cart with a grin on her face.

"Hi, Brenda," she said brightly.

Brenda was wearing a cute pink and white striped shirt and white shorts. She had her hair up in a high ponytail and her hands were covered in cotton candy.

"Hi, Cindy!" she said excitedly.

"I didn't know you worked here," Cindy said.

"I just started at the beginning of summer."

"Do you like it?"

"Yeah." Brenda looked around and then leaned in conspiratorially. "But some of the people who work here are crazy. You wouldn't believe it."

Cindy chuckled. "You'd be surprised."

"You came for the day?"

"Yes. My brother is filming stuff. We came to hang out and we'll check out some of the filming later."

Brenda's eyes grew wide. "Your brother works for the Escape! Channel?"

"Yup. Kyle Preston."

"He's your brother?"

From the way Brenda's eyes glazed over Cindy deduced that she'd found another one of her brother's admirers. It got old, but at least it wasn't as onerous as it used to be.

"That's the one," she said.

"Wow."

"If you'd like to meet him, I could arrange it."

Brenda actually squealed in excitement and it made Cindy smile. The girl had a rough home life, and if there was something Cindy could do to bring her happiness she gladly would. Even if it meant feeding her brother's already over-inflated ego.

Be nice, she reminded herself as she found herself slipping into the old mental habit of Kyle bashing.

A young woman dressed in a khaki colored uniform walked up to them.

"Becca! This is Cindy from my church, the one who solves all those mysteries I told you about."

Becca's eyes grew wide. "Wow! Are you investigating one here?" she asked.

Cindy shook her head. "We're just here to have some fun. A little later we're going to go see my brother film some stuff."

"Her brother's part of the Escape! Channel, too!" Brenda said excitedly.

Becca grinned. "Then he knows my sister, Bunni Sinclair."

"Oh my gosh! I met her in Las Vegas when Kyle was in the hospital!" Cindy said.

"Wait, mystery solving Cindy that Brenda knows is Kyle's sister Cindy that Bunni knows?" Becca asked.

Cindy nodded.

Becca bounced forward and threw her arms around her in a big hug. "It's so great to meet you!" she said.

"It's great to meet you, too," Cindy said.

A moment later Becca let go of her and stepped back. Becca fished a gold dollar coin out of her shirt pocket and handed it to Brenda. "Here, before I forget. We've had it in the cash register for ages."

"Thanks!" Brenda said, eyes wide. "That's my second one in a week." She glanced up. "Sorry, I collect the dollar coins," she said. "When Becca told me she had one I gave her a paper dollar to trade it in for me."

"I work at the Muffin Mansion," Becca said.

Cindy vaguely remembered seeing her there before.

"The Mansion has the best muffins!" Brenda enthused. "Particularly the seasonal ones. They have peppermint and a gingerbread with gumdrops in it."

Becca's eyes seemed to glaze over as Brenda was describing the muffins. "So much sugar," she whispered.

"Sugar?" Cindy asked.

"Where?" Becca asked, looking wildly around.

"Um, everywhere? The muffins, the cotton candy, lots of other places I'm sure," she said.

Becca sighed. "I can't have sugar."

"Because it makes her crazy, that's why," a man said. He seemed to come out of nowhere and he glared at Becca. "I figgered I'd find you here. Ye been told to stay away from the cotton candy girl," he said menacingly.

6

Becca balled her hands into fists at her side.

"I'm not harassing the cotton candy operator," she said defiantly. "I haven't once tried to get cotton candy out of her."

"That's true," Brenda said.

"Aye, but it's only a matter of time," Gibb said.

Cindy couldn't help but feel like she'd stepped into the middle of some sort of warped melodrama where Becca was both damsel in distress and somehow also the villain. The way Gibb talked made him sound like a pirate, but he seemed to have taken over the role of policeman.

Becca looked like she wanted to argue with him, but instead she sighed and trudged toward the Muffin Mansion.

"Is she okay?" Traci asked, concern clear in her voice. "Is that guy a problem?"

"Gibb isn't the problem. He's saving us all from Becca," Brenda said.

"From her?" Cindy asked, surprised.

"The way I hear it, her sugar allergy is super intense and it makes her go crazy and do insane things, scary things."

"That's terrifying," Lizzie said softly.

Cindy could only imagine what kind of awful things were going through the other woman's mind. Lizzie had a much more intimate view of insane and scary things than most people did.

"It seems like Gibb is the one who's responsible to make sure she doesn't get hold of any sugar," Brenda said. Brenda paused and suddenly her eyes grew wide. She was staring past Cindy at something behind her. "It's him!" she whispered.

Cindy turned and saw Kyle walking toward her. With him was Bunni Sinclair. Bunni waved. A moment later Cindy hugged her.

"It's good to see you again, especially under better circumstances," Cindy said.

"I know! I was so excited when I found out you lived here," Bunni said.

Bunni stepped back and gave Kyle a smile. It struck Cindy anew how much Bunni cared for her brother. She just wondered when Kyle would finally notice.

"We're off for the next hour-and-a-half," Kyle said. "We were coming over to see if Bunni's sister was free for lunch." He turned and looked at Traci and Geanie and gave them both smiles that were a bit strained.

Cindy couldn't blame him. The last time they'd all been together had not been a great experience.

"Hey," Geanie said, forcing a smile back.

Traci nodded.

"We just met Becca," Cindy said.

Bunni's eyes narrowed as she looked at the cotton candy cart.

"She didn't have any sugar, did she?"

"No," Brenda spoke up quickly.

"That's a relief," Bunni said.

"Kyle, I'd like you to meet some friends of mine," Cindy said. "This is Lizzie, Traci's younger sister."

"It's a pleasure to meet you," Kyle said warmly with a sincere smile.

He extended his hand and Lizzie shook it shyly.

"And this is Brenda, she's a friend from church," Cindy said.

Kyle walked around the cart so that he could offer Brenda his hand as well.

"Nice to meet you," he said.

Brenda stared at him for a second, not moving. Then, instead of shaking his hand, she launched herself forward and wrapped her arms around him in a tight hug.

"I'm a huge fan!" she squealed.

Kyle was even more taken aback than Cindy was. After a second, though, he hugged the girl back and patted her on the shoulder.

"In that case it's very nice to meet you," he said.

For an awkward couple of moments it looked like Brenda wasn't going to let go. She finally did, stepping away from Kyle and blushing fiercely.

To Kyle's credit, he seemed to recover quickly. Cindy couldn't help but wonder how many of his fans became a little too enthusiastic when meeting him.

"Bunni," Kyle said, "these are my friends, Geanie and Traci," he said. "This is Bunni, she works at the Escape Channel! with me."

The women shook hands all around. Cindy was surprised that Kyle had referenced Geanie and Traci as his friends and not hers. It did seem to go a long way to helping everyone relax.

"Would all of you be free for lunch?" Bunni asked.

"As long as we go on The Atomic Coaster first," Traci said.

"I love this ride," Kyle said, turning to look at it admiringly. "I've only thrown up on it twice."

"You can sit next to Bunni," Geanie said.

"And far away from the rest of us," Traci added.

He rolled his eyes then looked around as if suddenly remembering something.

"Where are all the guys?"

"Work," Geanie said.

Kyle smiled. "So, it's just me and a bevvy of beauties. Their loss."

Lizzie actually smiled at that.

"How about the rest of you go check on the ride while I go see if Becca is free?" Bunni said.

"Good idea," Kyle told her. "We'll meet you at the exit." He looked at Brenda. "Would you care to join us for lunch?"

Brenda sighed and shook her head. "I've already had my lunch break. I'm stuck with the cart for a couple more hours."

"Okay, well, hopefully I'll see you again," he said.

Brenda nodded, blushing again. "Definitely."

Suddenly the cotton candy cart seemed to come alive with a series of beeps and lights. A moment later it began rolling off on its own.

"Apparently it's time to move to a different location in the park. See you later," Brenda said. She gave them all a little wave and then turned to walk after the cart.

They got in line for the ride and Cindy found herself standing next to Kyle. "It's not nice breaking young girls' hearts," she said.

He suddenly turned serious. "Kids have crushes. Better that she have one on me than some slimeball who might want to take advantage of the situation."

"That's true. I hadn't thought of it that way," Cindy said.

Kyle started smiling again. "Besides, when I was her age if I had met Lynda Carter and she was cold or distant I would have been crushed."

She looked at him in surprise. "I didn't know you had a crush on Lynda Carter when we were kids."

"Wonder Woman? How could I not? I watched the reruns endlessly. She was beautiful and fearless and nothing could ever hurt her," he said, his smile faltering slightly.

A wave of sympathy washed over Cindy. She was beginning to see all the ways in which Lisa's death had affected Kyle. She didn't want to dwell on the negative, though, especially not right then.

"So, do you have a crush on Gal Gadot these days?"

"The current Wonder Woman? How could I not?" Kyle said with a smirk.

~

Jeremiah felt like he was missing something. G-d had told him to reread the prophets and he'd been doing just that for the past couple of weeks. He kept feeling like there was something he was supposed to learn, but so far nothing new was jumping out at him.

There was a knock on his door and he looked up as Marie entered. She stood there for a moment, staring at him.

"Yes?" he asked.

She frowned, clearly concentrating. "I don't know."

"You don't remember what you wanted to talk about?" he asked.

She shook her head slowly, a look of irritation replacing the confusion. She made a sound of disgust and turned to go, closing the door.

"Well, that was different," he said.

~

"I feel sick," Lizzie said as they made it to the exit of the coaster.

"It will pass in a couple of minutes," Kyle said reassuringly.

"I hope so," Cindy said.

She was feeling a little queasy herself.

Bunni and Becca were waiting for them at the exit.

"I jailbroke her," Bunni said.

"I was going on lunch break in half an hour and it's slow in the Mansion," Becca said.

"Where shall we eat?" Kyle asked.

"Poseidons is good if you're looking for a sit-down restaurant. It's right there," Becca said, pointing to a building about thirty feet away.

The outside of the building looked like an archaeological dig had been set up with some columns partially unearthed. The entryway looked like a hole carved out of a mound of dirt. A referee outside was dressed up like a 1930s archaeologist.

"Works for me," Kyle said. "How about everyone else?"

"Sure," Geanie said.

The rest, including Cindy, nodded. Becca led the way into the dig site and into the restaurant. They were surrounded by partially unearthed structures as the corridor wound downward. Eventually it emptied out into a stunning room that was part archaeological ruin and part giant aquarium. Fish swam by overhead and underfoot as well as through portions of the walls.

"Wow," Lizzie said.

"Amazing," Cindy said. She'd been to The Zone several times but never been in this restaurant before.

Despite the fact that there were several parties ahead of them, they were immediately seated at a large, round table in a secluded corner.

"It looks like they gave us the best table in the house," Kyle commented.

"Sometimes traveling with a celebrity can have its perks," Traci said, looking at him.

He shook his head.

"I'm pretty sure this had nothing to do with me. The maître d' only had eyes for Bunni," he said. "She's much more famous than I am."

"Stop," Bunni said. She sounded like she was blushing but with the blueish light in the restaurant it was impossible to tell.

"It's both of you," Becca said. "And it didn't hurt that I'm wearing my uniform which referees are never supposed to wear on rides or in restaurants unless they're escorting VIPs."

"To Becca," Geanie said, holding up an imaginary glass.

"Yay, Becca!" Cindy said, happy to give the credit to her instead of Kyle.

The waitress came over shortly to take their order. The entire menu was made up of fish dishes except for one lonely chicken dish. Cindy was surprised when Kyle ordered it.

"Why on earth would you order chicken at a seafood restaurant?" she asked.

"I don't eat fish," he said.

"Since when. You used to love fish," she said.

"Yeah, when I was a kid," he said, his voice suddenly strained.

"I remember you insisted on having tuna sandwiches for a whole month once," Cindy said.

It seemed odd to her since she had so many memories of him eating fish. Most people's palates expanded when they got older. For some reason Kyle's had shrunk.

"Can we please not talk about me eating fish?" Kyle said, a little too loudly and aggressively.

"Okay. I'm sorry," Cindy said, startled.

Everyone at the table stared as an uncomfortable silence descended. Kyle turned to look at her and she was surprised to see that he looked trapped and vulnerable.

Kyle dropped his eyes to the table. "Sorry, everyone."

"If you want to eat somewhere else, we can," Geanie finally said.

"No, it's not…" He stopped and heaved a sigh. He finally looked up. "When we went camping, the last time, something, uh happened."

Cindy's stomach suddenly did a somersault. She was not ready to discuss Lisa, particularly not after their last discussion of her in a nice restaurant at The Zone.

"Dad and Lisa used to go fishing early in the morning while Cindy and… Cindy started breakfast," he said.

Cindy noticed that he intentionally omitted referencing their mother.

"I went with them and they were going to teach me. I kept trying to cast the line. Well, it got tangled in trees, hit some rocks, everything but the water. Then I accidentally hooked Lisa in the hand. It wasn't bad, it was just a little snag. I felt awful, though. Well, she liked to tease. She could be almost mean about it sometimes, actually. She went on and on about how I must have thought she was a fish and how could I even consider killing and eating my sister for breakfast? She picked up one of the fish that dad caught and held it up next to her head and kept asking why the fish and she looked the same to me."

"Oh no," Cindy whispered.

"Yeah. So, later that day, I wanted to be like the big kids and jump off the cliff into the water. Lisa took me and she died. I killed my sister."

A tear slid down his cheek. He brushed it away roughly.

"I might have killed her, but I swore I'd never eat her. I haven't touched a fish since that day."

"That's really messed up," Lizzie said.

Bunni was openly crying and she grabbed Kyle's hand.

"You didn't kill her," Cindy said, grabbing Kyle's other hand.

"I don't think everyone agrees with you on that point," Kyle said.

Cindy thought he might be talking about himself since their mother had made it pretty clear she blamed Cindy. Unless in her insanity she had started blaming Kyle now, too.

The waitress reappeared and set two baskets of sourdough rolls on the table. Cindy stared at the rolls, struggling with what to say to her brother.

Kyle cleared his throat. "Well, on that happy note, how about the theming in here, pretty cool, isn't it?"

"I was just thinking we need to have an aquarium like this installed in one of the rooms of the house," Geanie said as she grabbed one of the rolls. "The only question is, which one?"

"A bathroom," Kyle said.

"What?" Cindy and the others all chorused.

"Hey, if it worked for Hearst Castle, I'm sure it would be perfect in Castle Coulter."

"It's hardly a castle," Geanie said. "And no thank you. I don't want fish watching me while I'm in the restroom."

"If it's just fish watching you that's the problem, maybe install an aviary instead," Kyle said with a smirk.

Geanie threw her roll at him. It hit him square in the chest with a thunk.

Just like that everyone was laughing and talking again. Cindy looked across the table and saw Becca bouncing up and down in her seat slightly. The other woman's fingers were wrapped tight around a roll and her eyes were darting around the table.

She's debating who to throw that thing at, Cindy thought to herself.

Before she could stop herself, Cindy grabbed her own roll and launched it at Becca. It bounced off the top of her head.

"Oh, sorry! I was aiming lower," Cindy said.

"You were aiming for my face?" Becca asked.

"No, like your chest area."

A wicked grin flickered across Becca's face. She flung her first roll at Cindy and snatched up another one which she threw at Traci.

Thirty seconds later there was no ammunition left as the waitress descended on them. The woman bent down and picked up a couple of the rolls that had ended up on the floor a few feet away. She straightened up and Cindy was sure they were about to get a lecture.

"Do you guys need a couple more baskets?" she asked instead.

"Yes, please," Geanie said with a grin.

As the waitress headed off Cindy stared at the others. "She's actually bringing us more? What just happened?"

"Rule one of The Zone," Becca said proudly. "Let players play."

~

Lunch had been a raucous affair the entire way through. Cindy had eaten several of the sourdough rolls which were amazingly good. She had managed to shove thoughts of their mother and Lisa out of her mind for the most part. It seemed like Kyle had, too.

They finally left the restaurant. Becca took them out a side door which led off field to the area where only those who worked there were supposed to go. They entered the park again in the Splash Zone where Kyle was supposed to be filming his next segment.

They were in an alleyway between two buildings. Two-thirds of the way down it was a cotton candy cart.

"We should tell Brenda to come by when her shift is over and watch some of the filming," Kyle said.

"That's sweet. I'm sure she'll be thrilled," Cindy said with a grin.

She looked at the cart but didn't see Brenda.

She must be crouched down behind the cart, Cindy thought.

They reached the cart and moved around it.

Traci stopped suddenly. She let out a sharp gasp. She raised her hand and pointed. Cindy looked.

"Oh no!" Cindy gasped.

There on the ground behind the cart, lying dead in a pool of blood, was a young woman. Cindy recognized her pink and white striped blouse and white shorts.

"No!" Cindy screamed as she dropped to her knees beside the body.

7

Mark was still trying to figure out why Brie Vargas had been killed. Since she had been killed in his backyard he was supposed to be sitting the case out. Every time he tried to focus on one of his other open cases, though, he thought of the look on Traci's face. He couldn't sit it out. He needed to help get this closed as soon as possible for her sake and his.

Liam slammed down his phone and stood up abruptly from his desk. He slowly walked around it to stand next to Mark.

Mark looked at his partner closely. Something was definitely wrong.

"What's eating you?" he asked.

"We just got the call. Another homicide."

"Not in my backyard, I hope," Mark said.

"No. In The Zone."

"That's new." Mark stood up and grabbed his jacket. "Okay, let's go check it out."

Liam laid a hand on Mark's shoulder.

"Traci and Cindy found the body," Liam said.

Mark froze. His guts twisted themselves into a knot at the thought.

"You have got to be kidding me," he said.

"Wish I was. You might want to go as a husband and not a detective."

"I'm going as both," Mark said fiercely.

Liam hesitated.

"What?" Mark snapped.

"I know it's not really my place, but I think that right now Traci needs you to be one or the other, not do a half-assed job trying to be both."

Mark bit back a sharp response. Liam was trying to look out for Traci and him. The other man didn't usually try to intervene like that, so Mark knew that he was serious. He was probably right, too. That was the devil of it.

"I need me to be both," he said.

That was also the truth. He couldn't be wholly one or the other in this situation.

"Fair enough," Liam said with a nod. "I'm driving."

Mark didn't argue. Most of the time Mark drove, but given how he was currently feeling, being behind the wheel might not be the best place for him.

"Fine," Mark growled. "Let's move."

As soon as they were in the car Liam briefed him on what little he'd heard. Mark then took the opportunity to call Jeremiah. One of them, at least, was going to need to be doing emotional triage while the other tried to solve this thing. Not that he didn't think Liam was perfectly capable, but in cases like this two heads, or even three, was a lot better than one.

"Given the time of day I'm fairly certain this isn't a social call," Jeremiah said, sounding less than thrilled.

"We got a body at The Zone. Our special ladies landed right in the middle of the mess."

"Of course they did," Jeremiah said with a sigh. "Cindy has the greatest knack for sniffing out trouble that I've ever seen. It's a wonder the government's never tried to recruit her."

"While I agree with everything you just said, it sounds like Traci had the honors this time," Mark told him.

There was silence and then a few unintelligible words.

"You swearing in Hebrew, rabbi?" Mark asked.

"Something like that," Jeremiah said. "I'll meet you there."

Jeremiah hung up and Mark put his phone back in his pocket.

"I'm planning on proposing to Rebecca on New Year's Eve," Liam said. "I know it's a bit of a cliché, but I want to start the new year as an engaged man."

"What?" Mark said.

"I'm going to ask Rebecca to marry me," Liam said.

"No, I heard what you said. Just, why bring this up now?"

"I don't know. Thinking about wives, I guess. Anyway, I wanted you to know."

"That's great," Mark said, struggling to force himself to be present in the car with Liam instead of racing ahead in his mind to what they were going to find at their destination. "At least you've already met her parents."

"Yeah. They're not entirely thrilled with the fact that I'm a cop, but at least they seemed to like me."

"That's good. And has she met your family?"

Liam fell silent.

Mark peered intently at his partner.

"I take it that's a 'no' on the family?" Mark asked.

"My family is…complicated," Liam said.

"Given what little I know of your gun-toting grandfather and your Bible-quoting grandmother I don't doubt it," Mark said. "Look, I know what everyone says, but at the end of the day she's marrying you, not your family. It would be nice if everyone got along, but sometimes you just have to cope."

"Yeah, well, some families are harder to get along with than others."

Mark turned to look at his partner. Liam looked tense and his jaw muscles were clenched. He was white-knuckling the steering wheel as though he was trying to choke the life out of it. Mark didn't know if his own stress was causing his imagination to run wild, but a sudden uneasy feeling twisted his guts around.

"There isn't something you should be telling me about them, is there? Like, you know, something that could become a problem for me if you get killed?"

"There should be no problems for you if I get killed. Just steer clear of them at the funeral if you can. I'm sure you and they would be happier that way."

"What, they have a thing against non-Irish guys or just cops?"

"Old prejudices run deep in parts of my family."

"You're making me feel all kinds of disturbed right now," Mark told him.

"I'm not meaning to."

"You know, it ended bad for me last time I didn't know enough about my partner."

"I know," Liam said quietly. "But believe me, you don't have to worry."

Something in his tone, though, said quite the opposite. Mark had the distinct impression that he should worry quite a bit.

"Well, one thing's for sure, New Year's Eve is going to be a heck of a night for all of us," Mark said.

Liam scowled. "You talking about Joseph and Geanie?"

"Yeah."

"What's the plan on that?"

"The problem is, we don't have one."

"Cutting things mighty close, don't you think?"

"Too close," Mark agreed.

"You need help?"

"With the way the end of this year is going I think I need all the help I can get," Mark said.

"You know, I think you need a vacation. You and Traci could use it."

"I know. Things are just a bit crazy right now."

"When are they not?" Liam asked. "I mean, seriously?"

"You're right," Mark said with a sigh. "They're always crazy."

"Now that we've established that, what more have you found out about this secret society?"

"A big, fat nothing."

"Then how do you know it even exists?"

"You're joking, right?" Mark asked incredulously.

"Hear me out. How do you know it isn't one sick guy who has set up this whole elaborate charade as a way to get others to kill people for his amusement?"

"It's an interesting theory. Even if it's just one guy behind it, or heck even two or three, he or they seem to be very well connected and on the ball. Plus, we have too many people that know somebody or at least seem to. That's an awful lot of rich, influential people to try and fool."

"How many?" Liam asked.

"How many what?"

"How many people do we know have been recruited?"

"Cartwright, he killed his secretary slash mistress to get in. Ivan, he killed the stripper. And whoever has been in contact with Joseph since Ivan's death. So, we know the club at least had those three. One's dead. One's in jail. And one is out there somewhere making our lives difficult."

"That's it?"

"Isn't that enough?"

"Hear me out," Liam said. "Two guys in this area have murdered women to be in this little club. It's supposedly a very influential group. Why would it only be recruiting in this area?"

"It wouldn't," Mark said. "At bare minimum it would spread out a few miles, probably start incorporating Los Angeles. I mean, if ever there were rich, unscrupulous people just waiting for some exclusive opportunity, it would be the ones who live there."

"So, as I see it there are two possibilities. Either this is a small organization with a small sphere of influence and a tiny focus or this is a larger organization with a much greater reach. If it's the latter-"

"Then there should be a lot more dead women out there that were murdered because of this thing and we have to expand the scope of our investigation," Mark interrupted.

"Exactly. I think we need to reach out to other departments and see if they have any cases that might indicate this group was behind them."

"It would help if we could narrow this down to wives and mistresses of rich guys," Mark said. "Unfortunately, in our experience rich isn't necessarily a requirement as much as ambition and potential are."

"And Ivan murdered a stripper who had no ties to him other than they were both at that bachelor party," Liam said.

"We could as easily be looking for prostitutes as society wives."

"Yes."

"That's going to be a lot of cases to slog through," Mark said.

"All the more reason to get started now."

"Yeah, but it's going to have to wait," Mark said as they arrived at The Zone.

Mark and Liam got out of the car.

"Remember when we used to have nice, simple cases that were open and shut, none of this dragging on forever business?" Mark said.

"No, and neither do you."

~

Cindy let out a sob of relief when she saw Mark and Liam walking toward them. She turned quickly to Traci who was sitting on a bench next to Geanie, each of them leaning slightly on the other. Lizzie was sitting on Traci's other side, gently rubbing her back.

"Mark's here," Cindy said.

Traci got up and ran to her husband. She threw her arms around his neck and clung to him as she cried.

Liam went immediately to the body, not even bothering to greet any of them. That was fine with Cindy. She was still in shock and grief kept hitting her in waves. Over and over in her head she kept thinking that if they'd found a way to make Brenda go to lunch with them she'd still be alive. Part of her mind kept telling her that wasn't necessarily true. If someone had been targeting Brenda they would have just waited.

Who would possibly want to hurt Brenda? Cindy thought. It was unthinkable. Brenda was sweet and kind. She was just a kid with her whole life ahead of her.

Liam looked up from his examination of the body.

"Does anyone know her?" he asked.

Cindy nodded.

"Yes," Becca said. "At least I think so. I haven't been able to see her face, but I think it's Brenda." Becca was sitting with Bunni, the two sisters holding each other. Kyle was standing nearby.

"Do you think you can come over here and take a closer look?" Liam asked.

Becca stood up and approached the body a little unsteadily.

"Take your time," Liam said gently.

Cindy didn't want to look, but it was as though she couldn't look away. She didn't want to see that vacant look in Brenda's eyes that meant she was gone. Still she walked over as Becca crouched down next to the body. Liam gently pulled back the dead girl's hair.

"It's not her!" Becca said.

Cindy sagged in relief. Even as she thanked God that it wasn't Brenda she prayed for the family of whoever this girl was.

"Who is she, do you know?"

Becca nodded slowly.

"She's new. I don't know her name. I've only seen her a couple of times."

"Okay," Liam said. "Can you tell me who would know?"

"Martha, her supervisor. Or Brenda, probably."

"So, if this isn't Brenda, where is she?" Liam asked.

Before Becca could answer there was a high-pitched scream behind them. Cindy turned and saw Brenda standing there, a look of horror on her face.

Cindy jumped to her feet and ran to Brenda. She spun the other girl around so she couldn't see the body and wrapped her in a tight hug.

"Thank you, God, for keeping Brenda safe," she whispered.

"What happened? What's going on?" Brenda cried. "Is Theresa dead?"

"Is that her name, Theresa?" Cindy asked.

"Yes. She was watching my cart while I was on lunch break," Brenda said.

Cindy bit her lip. A million thoughts were racing through her mind. Had Theresa been the intended victim or Brenda? Or was it all just a random act of violence? In her gut she didn't think it was, although she couldn't say for sure why she felt that way.

Cindy looked at the two detectives. Mark still had his hands full with Traci.

"Liam!" she called out.

Liam stood up and came over.

"The girl who was watching the cart for Brenda here was named Theresa," Cindy said, trying to keep her voice as calm and measured as she could.

"When did she take over from you?" Liam asked.

"Just under an hour ago. I was coming back," Brenda said, her voice cracking.

Becca came over and put her arms around Brenda. She met Cindy's eyes.

"I've got her," Becca said.

Cindy nodded slowly and let go before stepping back. She walked over to Mark and Traci. Traci had stopped crying at least. Cindy's heart ached for her. This day was not turning out to be the fun distraction it was supposed to be.

"Hey, good news. It's not Brenda."

Cindy winced as she realized how that must sound. Someone was still dead, and it sounded like it didn't matter to her since she hadn't known her. That wasn't the case, but she figured Mark and Traci understood what she meant.

"It was the girl that was covering the cart during Brenda's lunch break," Cindy said. "Brenda's over there and she's okay."

"That's a relief," Mark said. "At least the dead girl's a stranger to us."

Traci started crying anew.

"What's wrong?" Mark asked.

Traci shook her head.

"What?" he pressed.

"Sooner or later our luck's going to run out," she said.

A chill ran down Cindy's spine.

"What do you mean?" Cindy asked.

"One of these days it's going to be someone we know, probably one of the six of us."

8

Jeremiah felt like he might be sick as he raced to The Zone. Geanie had called to let him know that they'd found a body and Cindy believed it was Brenda's. He was hoping and praying that they were wrong. Brenda was one of the kids he'd been trapped with at Green Pastures. He'd seen her off and on the last couple of years. She still called herself one of the Rabbi's Rangers. It would gut him if something had happened to her. If she was dead he'd personally tear her killer limb from limb.

Once he'd made it to the park and explained why he was there a referee directed him to the area. He slipped past a temporary barricade that had been put up. Moments later he spotted Cindy. He'd started toward her when he saw Brenda talking to Liam. Relief surged through him and he walked straight to Brenda.

She turned, saw him, and ran toward him. She threw her arms around him and began to cry softly.

"Are you okay?" he asked.

She nodded slightly and looked up at him.

"It could have been me," she whispered.

"But it wasn't. You are alive and well and that's a blessing," he said. "Do you need me to call anyone?"

"I already called Sarah. She's coming over."

"Sarah, the one I know?"

She nodded. "Rabbi's Rangers take care of each other."

72

He couldn't help but feel a swell of pride. It was amazing how the kids from Green Pastures had stayed so close to each other.

Brenda finally let go of him and together they walked over to join the others. Cindy looked relieved to see him. Kyle managed a wan smile. Traci and Mark were standing slightly apart. It was clear that Mark was trying to keep her calm. What was unclear at a glance was whether or not he was succeeding.

"Hey, Jeremiah, good to see you," Kyle said.

"Kyle," he said, nodding his head.

Kyle turned to Bunni and the young woman with her.

"Bunni, I don't know if you met him in Las Vegas, but this is my future brother-in-law, Jeremiah. Jeremiah, this is Bunni Sinclair, she's a coworker. And this is her sister, Becca, who works here at the park."

"Good to see you again, Bunni. Nice to meet you, Becca," Jeremiah said.

He reached out and shook hands with both of them. With the introductions officially out of the way he put a hand on Cindy's back.

"Are you okay?" he asked her.

"Now that I know Brenda is alive and well, I'm much better," Cindy said.

"Me, too."

Several police officers were on the scene and Liam broke away from them to approach the group.

"There's a breakroom a short distance from here. It's been cleared and I'd like you to go wait there." He glanced over at Mark and Traci. "All of you," he said firmly.

"Will do," Jeremiah said.

"I'll take everyone there," Brenda said quickly.

"I appreciate it," Liam said. He glanced again at Mark and Traci.

It was easy to tell that Liam was worried about them. From what Jeremiah had observed in the last day, Liam was right to worry.

A minute later they were all in a medium sized room, sitting at a couple of tables. They were away from prying eyes, but Jeremiah felt it best to continue to give Mark and Traci some space. Brenda and Geanie were at a table. Becca started grabbing coffee for everyone. Jeremiah found himself sharing another table with Cindy, Kyle, and Bunni.

Becca had just finished handing him a cup of coffee when the door to the breakroom opened. In walked a guy and a girl. He had sun bleached hair and she was a redhead. Jeremiah guessed them to be somewhere around nineteen or twenty. They both looked upset.

Becca gave a little yelp and bounded toward them. She threw her arms around the girl and they hugged for a moment. Then Becca brought them back to the table. Kyle and Bunni both nodded at the newcomers.

"Candace and Josh, allow me to introduce you to Cindy and Jeremiah," Becca said. "Cindy found the… found her. Jeremiah is her fiancé. Cindy, Jeremiah, these are my friends Candy and Josh."

"How do you do?" Jeremiah asked, rising to shake their hands.

"It's a dark day," Josh said. "Is there anything that any of you need?"

"Hi, Candy!" Brenda said, also moving to hug Candace.

"The theme park sent you to take care of us?" Cindy asked, her voice skeptical.

Becca glanced at Josh who nodded at her in a knowing way.

"It's okay," Josh told Becca. He turned and focused his attention on Jeremiah and Cindy. "I'm Josh Hanson. My parents own The Zone. They are unfortunately on their way to a conference in Europe along with my older brother. They'll all be turning around and heading back as soon as they can. Until they do, I'm here to represent the park. This is my girlfriend."

"I started out at The Zone as a cotton candy operator," Candace said, giving Brenda a small smile. "I can't believe what's happening. Is everyone here alright?"

"Here, sit down and I'll get you some soda," Becca said, indicating the table adjacent to Jeremiah and Cindy's.

Candace and Josh sat down while Becca retrieved sodas from a refrigerator on the far side of the room.

Jeremiah could tell that Mark was watching, but the detective made no move to join the conversation. As soon as Candace was seated, Brenda sat next to her, scooting her chair close.

"Candace really helped me out my first week on the job a few months ago before she headed off to Florida for college," Brenda told Jeremiah.

"I know what it's like to be the new ref and to deal with cotton candy in ninety-degree heat," Candace said with a smile. Her smile quickly faded, though. "Are you okay?" she asked Brenda.

Brenda nodded slowly. "I just can't believe Theresa is dead." Tears welled up in her eyes. "She isn't even the one who's been giving me breaks this week."

"Who is?" Cindy asked.

Jeremiah could tell that since she knew that Brenda was okay, Cindy's mind was busy working on figuring out what happened to Theresa.

"Brie has been giving me breaks, but I heard she didn't show up to work today."

That got Mark's attention. He rocketed to his feet and came over. "Brie Vargas?" he asked quietly.

"Yes, do you know her?" Brenda asked.

"I should have recognized the shirt," Mark muttered to himself, staring at Brenda's pink and white striped uniform shirt.

"What is it?" Cindy asked quickly.

Mark hesitated, but then finally gave in with a shake of his head.

"Brie was found dead yesterday morning," he said. "She was murdered."

Everyone who worked for the park gasped in shock. Jeremiah wished he was surprised, but he really wasn't. Traci began to cry again and Mark returned to her. Lizzie sat next to her sister looking miserable and helpless.

Brenda, Becca, and Candace clung together. Brenda cried while the other two just stared in glassy-eyed shock.

"Who would do such a thing?" Josh asked, clenching his fists in anger.

"I don't know," Jeremiah confessed.

Josh stood up and started for the door.

"Where are you going?" Jeremiah asked sharply.

"I'm heading to operations, and I'm closing the park," Josh said.

"I don't think that's a good idea just yet," Jeremiah said.

"Then I'm going to shut down the remaining cotton candy carts and bring the operators here for protection,"

Josh said in a decisive tone. "Where was Brie killed?" he asked.

"About a block from her home," Jeremiah said, unwilling to share more than that for the moment.

"Okay. I'm also going to call in those who aren't working."

"Why?" Kyle asked, brow furrowing.

"Because someone's targeting our cotton candy operators and until we find out who and why none of them are safe," Josh said.

~

Cindy watched as Josh left the room. He might be young, but he was smart and willing to take responsibility. She'd had her doubts when he and his girlfriend had first arrived, but he seemed more than capable of handling things.

She turned her attention to the others in the room. Becca and Brenda were holding on to each other and Bunni moved over to be with her sister. Candace gave up her chair and moved over to their table, sitting down in the seat next to Kyle.

"Candace, or is it Candy?" Cindy asked her.

"Candace, but a lot of people in The Zone know me as Candy. Whichever is fine," she said.

"Okay," Cindy said. "You say you used to be a cotton candy operator?"

"Yes, the summer before last. It was my first job here at the park," she said.

There was a question burning in her mind, but Cindy didn't know how best to proceed. She didn't want to freak the girl out any more than she already was. Candace stared back at her and slowly the shock began to fade from her eyes.

"You're wondering if this is about me," Candace finally said.

Cindy nodded.

"I don't see how it could be. I mean, I've worked three jobs here since that one plus two jobs out in Florida at Zone World. If this is about me someone has seriously outdated information." Candace paused and then a shadow seemed to pass across her face. She frowned as though in concentration.

"What is it?" Cindy pushed.

"It is the role I'm best known for," she admitted. "But no one would expect me to be doing that right now."

Something just didn't feel right to Cindy. Two dead cotton candy sellers in two days couldn't be a coincidence. Why had they been killed? Why had Brenda been spared? Had it been simply a matter of timing or was there something more that connected the other two girls?

"How many cotton candy sellers are there?" Cindy asked, half to herself and half to Candace.

"I don't know how many there are right now. I know during peak season there's about eight."

"There's seven right now," Brenda said, overhearing them.

"Is that including the two?" Cindy asked, not wanting to really finish that sentence.

Brenda nodded soberly.

"So, that leaves four currently unaccounted for," Cindy said. "Do you know if Theresa and Brie had anything in common? Were they friends outside of work?"

"I'm not sure," Brenda said.

Brenda looked down at her phone.

"Sarah's at the park and wants to know where we are."

"Tell me what she looks like and I'll go get her," Becca said, standing up.

"I can get her," Brenda said.

"You're not going anywhere right now," Jeremiah said.

It was clear from the tone of his voice that he was trying hard to be gentle while still being firm enough that she wouldn't question him. It worked because Brenda nodded.

Brenda pulled a picture of Sarah up on her phone and showed it to Becca.

"I'll walk with you," Cindy volunteered.

They hurried outside the room and made their way back toward the crime scene.

"Are you okay?" Cindy asked.

"I'm worried for my friends," Becca said.

"We'll find whoever did this."

"Yes, we will," Becca said, a hard edge to her voice. "My sister tells me you solve a lot of mysteries, stop a lot of bad guys."

"I do my best," Cindy said.

"Maybe there's another mystery you can help me out with," Becca said.

"What?"

"How dumb is your brother?"

The question took Cindy by surprise and she gave a short, hard laugh before she could stop herself.

"He can be pretty dumb, why?"

"Bunni's in love with him and he's oblivious."

"I've noticed," Cindy said. "I guess maybe he just needs time to finish getting over his ex-fianceé."

"It's been almost two years."

"Has it?" Cindy asked in surprise. So much had happened since then that at times it just seemed like a couple of months. At other times it felt like a lifetime ago.

"I don't want her to get hurt. She's not exactly the type to make the first move and even if she did, I'm afraid it would end badly."

"It's nice that you care about her so much."

"Of course, she's my sister."

"Well, to try and answer your question, I don't know. My brother can be more than a bit dense sometimes. He probably just needs some kind of a nudge to realize that Bunni is the perfect girl for him."

"A little nudge with a sledgehammer," Becca muttered.

It couldn't hurt, Cindy thought to herself.

~

Jeremiah wished that Cindy hadn't volunteered to go with Becca, but he kept reminding himself that neither of them were being targeted.

Kyle's phone rang and he got up and moved to the corner of the room before answering it. He came back a minute later and looked at Bunni.

"The director wanted to know what was going on and how long we'd be," he said.

"What did you tell him?" she asked.

"I told him a young girl was dead and to have some freaking sympathy. I told him to send the crew home for the day and if the boss has a problem he can take it up with me."

"You did the right thing," Jeremiah said before he could stop himself.

"It was the obvious thing," Kyle said, clearly upset.

"Kyle, don't worry. We're going to find who did this," Jeremiah told him.

Kyle looked up at him and there was raw pain in his eyes. "That doesn't make her any less dead," he said, anger filling his voice.

Jeremiah took a deep breath. "No, but we can stop it from happening to someone else."

"You weren't anywhere near here earlier today when this happened," Kyle said.

"No, I wasn't," Jeremiah said, not sure what Kyle was getting at.

Kyle stood there, looking down at him, hands clenched at his side.

"Cindy found her. She finds a lot of dead people. I don't know why. For a while I thought it was because of you, that somehow having you in her life was causing her to engage in risky behavior or that you were exposing her to bad elements or something. I went back over all the articles I could find about every crime she's solved, and you're always there, even if you manage not to be mentioned by name."

Jeremiah stood up. He needed to say something before this spun out of control.

"I-"

Kyle held up a hand, cutting him off. "I realize now it's not you. You're not the reason all these bad things keep happening to my sister." Tears sprang into Kyle's eyes. "You're the reason that she's surviving them. Thank you."

Kyle lurched forward and threw his arms around Jeremiah, hugging him tight. Jeremiah froze for a moment, trying to register what was happening. Then he hugged the other man back.

"I'm so grateful you're in her life," Kyle said. "I don't know what she'd do without you."

Jeremiah struggled with what to say. Before he could come up with an answer the door flew open. They both turned to look as a girl in a pink and white striped blouse raced into the room, sobbing.

9

Mark nearly fell out of his chair when he saw Kyle hug Jeremiah. For a split second he'd actually thought that Kyle was attacking him instead. When the girl ran into the room crying, though, that took all his attention. From her uniform he guessed she had to be one of the other cotton candy sellers. She saw Brenda and made a beeline for her and collapsed into her arms crying.

"I'll be back," Mark told Traci.

He stood up and walked over next to the girls. He was about to give his normal introduction but thought better of it. Instead he crouched down.

"Hello. My name is Mark and I'm a detective," he said. "I'm very sorry for what's happened here."

"I'm Joy," the girl whispered.

That's ironic, Mark thought to himself.

"I take it you're a cotton candy girl?"

She nodded.

The door opened again and Josh returned. "The park is closing. I see Joy made it here okay."

Mark nodded.

"I've called the other three. Lisa and Jennifer will be here shortly. Megan is visiting family in Virginia apparently, so she should be safe I would think."

"Good," Mark said. Four potential targets to keep an eye on was better than five.

"You really think all our cotton candy operators are targets?" Josh asked.

"Until we can find anything else that ties the two victims together we have to assume that the others are in danger. Two victims who work at a place as big as this could maybe be a coincidence. But two victims with the same job killed hours apart? That's a pattern."

"I can't even imagine who would do such a thing," Josh said.

Mark could. Years of being a cop had shown him just how monstrous people could be. The only real question in his mind was the motive for the killings. Was it a serial killer with something against cotton candy or girls in pink striped blouses? While anything was possible that seemed rather farfetched. Serial killers often had a type, but this was just way too specific. Maybe the killer had been trying to kill a specific cotton candy operator but got the wrong one the first time.

Given that the first girl had been killed in his backyard, that seemed odd. That implied that either the killer knew where she lived or had followed her from work. Either way he would have plenty of opportunities to see her face and know she was the wrong girl.

"What is it?" Jeremiah asked.

Mark turned to look at him. He nodded his head slightly and Jeremiah followed him to the corner of the room. He lowered his voice so only the rabbi could hear him.

"In your other life, did you ever mistake a target? Say you followed someone and afterward you realized they weren't who you thought they were?"

"You mean, did I get a good look at them only after I killed them?" Jeremiah asked bluntly.

"Yes."

"No."

"Okay," Mark said, taking a deep breath. "But you were a pro, highly trained. Is it possible that somebody killed the girl at my place because they mistook her for the one here?"

"The girl at your house had short, blond hair and was about five feet seven inches tall. The girl here has longer brown hair and is five feet tall. Even in the dark an amateur could tell that the two girls looked nothing alike."

"Except for their clothes."

"Except for their clothes," Jeremiah said.

"What does that have us looking for?" Mark asked.

"Someone who only knows the occupation of the target, not the identity."

"I was afraid you were going to say something like that," Mark muttered. "If that's the case, the other girls are in danger."

"Yes," Jeremiah agreed. "We have to assume for now that they are."

"So, other than being a sicko, what reason does someone have to kill the girls who work that job?"

"Off the top of my head they could be trying to make some sort of statement or have some sort of fixation."

"Maybe. What kind of statement?" Mark asked.

Jeremiah shook his head. "We'd probably have to run this theory by Josh and Candace to figure that out."

"Is there anything else we're not thinking of?" Mark asked. He really wasn't looking forward to discussing this with a couple of eighteen-year-olds, no matter who they were.

"It's possible that the killer is looking for a specific girl but has no idea which one."

"That makes no sense, though," Mark pointed out. "I mean, if someone has a grudge against one of them, they know who she is. Even if it's a hired gun, they get names, pictures."

"Except when they don't," Jeremiah said.

"When would they not?"

"When whoever wants them dead doesn't know that information. For example, what if someone thinks a cotton candy operator might have seen or overheard something she shouldn't. One or more people are talking or engaged in something illicit and glance up just in time to see a girl with a cart disappearing. They might not know who she was, but they know where she works."

"And what she wears," Mark muttered.

"Of course, if that's the case, we have a big problem," Jeremiah said.

"The killer won't rest until they're all dead, just to make sure he got the right one." The whole thing was going to get uglier fast. Mark could feel it in his bones. "So, all we have to do is get the girls to talk, find out which one of them has seen something she wasn't meant to."

"It's possible the girl doesn't even know," Jeremiah said. "She might not have even actually seen or heard anything. You know how paranoid criminals can get."

"Yeah, almost as paranoid as spies, but without as much to hide," Mark said.

"I think I resent that remark," Jeremiah said.

"You resemble that remark."

Jeremiah smiled faintly.

The door opened and Cindy and Becca entered with a girl he was sure he'd seen at some point around the synagogue. That had to be Sarah. Sarah ran forward and hugged Brenda fiercely.

Mark glanced back at Jeremiah who was also watching.

"I won't let anyone hurt those girls," he said, voice low and menacing.

"With you around I'm sure they're going to be safe," Mark said. "Right at this moment, though, I think they could probably use the rabbi more than the other."

Jeremiah nodded, clearly taking his point. The rabbi moved over and both girls embraced him. As Mark watched Jeremiah whispering words of comfort to the two girls it struck him that the rabbi would make a good father. His own twins were lucky to have Jeremiah as an uncle. And if the worst happened, they'd be lucky to have him as a father.

Mark froze as he realized the dark turn his thoughts had taken. He and Traci had already decided that if something happened to them they'd want Joseph and Geanie to raise the twins. He hadn't realized until that moment just how worried he was about the couple with all the secret society craziness going on. What if something happened to the four of them and it did fall upon Jeremiah and Cindy to raise his children?

He shook his head fiercely, trying to dispel the creeping darkness that was threatening to overtake him. It was natural that he was being morbid given that he had found the murdered girl in his backyard. It drove home the fact that death could come anywhere at any time.

He forced himself to take some deep, calming breaths. He wouldn't be any use to anyone if he fell apart while making up imaginary problems.

~

Jeremiah couldn't help but feel protective of Brenda and Sarah. After all, they were two of the kids who had been with him at Green Pastures. They'd survived that and they would survive this. His heart ached for them, though. They'd seen too much darkness in their young lives, and he wished there was something he could do to take that away. Some wounds, though, only G-d could heal. He prayed over them and with them along with the other girl, Joy, as the rest moved quietly about the room.

Still he managed to keep an eye on the others as well. They really needed to get Traci out of there. She was at the breaking point. Mark was also having a rough time of it and it was clear that he was brooding over something. Whatever it was, Jeremiah didn't think it was necessarily about the case at hand.

Other officers had begun circulating, collecting information. There was a lot to gather. Too much. They needed to thin out the group some. He managed to catch Liam's eye and the detective made his way over to him.

"I think we need to send some people home," Jeremiah said with a nod toward Traci.

"Ordinarily I wouldn't, but nothing about this is ordinary," Liam said. "I'll take care of it."

Five minutes later Traci, Lizzie, Geanie, and Cindy were leaving. Two police officers were with them and would be escorting them to Geanie's. Mark looked relieved which made sense. He'd been trying to split his attention between his wife and his job and not doing a great job of it.

Kyle and Bunni were released as well and left to meet up with the director and the rest of the cast and crew for the television special. There was no immediate reason to believe they had even a remote connection to what was going on. Despite what Kyle had said earlier Jeremiah still felt himself relax when Cindy's brother was out of sight. He wasn't sure if he would ever be completely comfortable around Kyle or vice versa. They'd made a start, though. Only G-d knew where it would go from there.

That left Mark, Liam, Sarah, the Zone people, and him. It was clear that there was no way Sarah was leaving Brenda's side until she knew her friend was okay. That could prove to be problematic since they didn't know whether or not Brenda and the other cotton candy operators were in danger.

Two more girls arrived, both in regular clothes. They were introduced as Jennifer and Lisa. Jeremiah noted that Candace hugged Lisa when she came in. After a couple of moments Mark drew everyone's attention.

"Brenda, Joy, Lisa, Jennifer I need you to all do some thinking. Over the past two weeks have any of you seen or heard anything out of the ordinary while you were working or wearing your costume?"

"We don't wear costumes. We wear uniforms," Brenda said, still clearly a little dazed.

"Okay, uniforms. So, here at work or going back and forth. Is there anything, even the slightest thing out of place, that you can think of?" Mark asked.

The girls all looked blank and slowly shook their heads.

"Brenda," Jeremiah said.

The girl turned her attention to him.

"Did you notice anyone acting like they wanted privacy?"

She wrinkled her brow as she thought. "I don't think so."

"Some people find quiet places when they're taking phone calls," Candace said. "We usually think they're just trying to hear the other person. Did anyone like that look especially furtive or like they wanted to be left alone?"

Jeremiah nodded approvingly. Candace had a good head on her shoulders.

There was silence for a long moment as the four girls thought. Finally Lisa spoke up.

"I saw two men arguing. They looked a bit scary and I got out of there fast," she said.

"Do you know what they looked like?" Mark asked.

"All I can tell you was that they were arguing in Spanish."

"Could you make out what they were saying?" Mark asked.

"No, my high school Spanish isn't that good," Lisa said.

"I saw a guy stuff a big wad of bills in his pocket a couple of days ago," Brenda said. "He seemed really anxious about it."

"I turned a corner on my way to the cantina for lunch yesterday and two guys took off running," Joy said. "I thought it was a bit odd, but I thought maybe they were in a hurry to get somewhere."

"I saw a lot of people on cell phones, but nothing that seemed weird," Jennifer offered.

Mark sighed. It wasn't a lot to go on and the detective's tension was palpable. Jeremiah just continued to sit, trying to be unobtrusive as he mulled over what each of the girls had said. There really wasn't much to go on.

"Did either Theresa or Brie mention seeing anything odd to any of you?" Liam asked.

All the girls shook their heads.

~

"So much for our relaxing day," Geanie said as she walked into her house.

Cindy nodded as she carefully watched Traci. She was really worried about her. Traci hadn't said a word on the drive back from The Zone.

They found Joseph in the kitchen staring off into space. He jumped when Geanie put her hand on his shoulder.

"You scared me," he said.

"I'm going to go upstairs and lie down for a while," Traci said.

"Do you need anything?" Cindy asked anxiously.

"No, I just need to rest I think."

Traci left and Cindy stared anxiously after her.

"I'll go be with her. I know what it's like to be traumatized by something like this," Lizzie said.

Lizzie left the room.

"I'm worried about Traci," Cindy said.

"So am I," Geanie said.

"I'm worried about you," Joseph told Geanie bluntly.

Cindy looked closely at her friend and realized that he looked more scared than she could ever remember seeing him.

"I'm going to be okay," Geanie said.

"We don't know that. These guys don't play around. We need a plan, a way out." He glanced around. "Where are Jeremiah and Mark?"

"They're still at the park helping out with the murder investigation."

Joseph scowled. "I need them here, dealing with this."

Cindy forced herself to smile. "We don't need them. Not when the three of us are equal to any challenge life could throw at us."

"That's right," Geanie said. "Let's put our heads together and figure this out."

"I have figured it out," he said.

"Then enlighten us," Geanie said.

"We're leaving the country tonight."

10

"What?" Cindy and Geanie blurted out together.

"We leave the country. I don't know how extensive this group's reach is, but I'm sure I can find a place where they won't come looking for us," Joseph said.

Cindy stared at him in shock as she realized that he was being serious.

"You can't just leave, run away," she said.

"Why not?" he asked. "We're talking about Geanie's life. There's nothing I wouldn't do to protect her."

"Honey, I don't want to go. We can't let someone chase us from our home," Geanie said.

"Sure we can. This is just a house. You are my home, my everything. Wherever you are is home."

Cindy could feel tears welling up in her eyes and she didn't know how Geanie was keeping it together.

"Listen to me," Geanie said, grabbing hold of Joseph. "We didn't run when that psycho tried to kill me and sabotage our wedding. We didn't run when those men kidnapped Clarice's puppies and killed people here in the house. Our friends are here. Our lives are here. Our *doctors* are here."

The last seemed like an odd thing to say. Before Cindy could comment, though, Joseph stood up. He wrapped Geanie in a bear hug.

"I love you so much. You're right. Now is not the time for running."

"Now that we've got that settled, why don't we set about figuring out how to take these guys down?" Cindy said.

Geanie turned to look at Cindy and burst out laughing.

"What's so funny?" Cindy asked.

"You," Geanie said, laughing harder.

"I'm not being funny," Cindy protested.

Joseph let go of Geanie and turned to Cindy. She was shocked to see that he was smiling.

"Yes, you are," Joseph said, unable to hold back a small laugh.

"What?"

Geanie giggled some more. "You said 'take these guys down' like it was the most normal thing in the world. When we first met, you were scared of your own shadow. And now you're…"

"Rambo," Joseph finished.

"Exactly!" Geanie crowed.

"I'm not Rambo," Cindy protested. She felt the corners of her mouth twitch upward. "But I am marrying him."

They all three dissolved into helpless laughter. As they held onto each other Cindy couldn't help but think that this was the best way to fight the darkness. You had to laugh at it.

~

Jeremiah couldn't help but wonder how Cindy and the others were doing. Things were wrapping up at The Zone. All the cotton candy operators were being given police protection. In an abundance of caution Mark also assigned police protection to Candace since she used to hold that job. Neither he nor the detective was convinced her being home on winter break from college had anything to do with what was going on.

It turned out that Candace had quite the reputation in the park. Surprisingly it had almost nothing to do with who her boyfriend was and everything to do with her. Given her storied history, complete with urban legends about her getting chased through the park by a psychopath, it just made sense to keep an eye on her as well.

She and Josh were huddled together talking near him. He was the only one close enough to hear what they were saying.

"I don't like this," Candace said. "I don't want police following me."

"It's no big deal," Josh said.

"How can you say that?" she asked.

"Because I've been through it."

"What? When?"

"A few years ago. My mom had a stalker and we had police protection for a couple of weeks because of that."

Candace's face clouded with concern.

"Your mom had a stalker? I never knew that."

Josh shrugged.

"She's actually had like half a dozen, but he was the only one who was a problem."

Candace stared at him with a look of horror on her face. It was clear that something like that was totally outside her own experience.

They come from two completely different worlds. Like Cindy and I, Jeremiah couldn't help but think.

He could tell from the way that Josh looked at her that he was just as in love with Candace as Jeremiah himself was with Cindy. They might not always have an easy road ahead of them, but he felt confident that they could work it out.

"The focus should be the girls who are currently cotton candy vendors, not me," Candace said.

"The focus is on them," Jeremiah said. "But if there is even the slightest possibility that the killer has even heard of you precautions have to be taken. And given what I've heard in the last hour if this guy is in any way connected with The Zone he's heard of you."

Candace flushed at that while Josh turned pale.

"You don't think it could be one of the referees, the people who work here, do you?" Josh asked.

"We can't rule it out at the moment," Jeremiah said.

"That would be terrible. We're all like family," Josh said.

"Maybe to you," Jeremiah said. "But not everyone might feel that way."

And not all families get along, he thought with a fleeting moment of sadness.

Josh's cell rang and he quickly answered.

"Yes. Okay, thanks."

He pocketed the phone and turned to address the room.

"The park's officially closed for the day. It's going to take about another half hour to get all the players out. There's going to be a meeting of the referees off field in an hour. I need to be able to tell them something. Rumors are already flying all over the place."

"Okay," Mark said.

"I'll handle the meeting with him," Liam volunteered.

"Thank you," Mark said, looking immensely relieved. "And make sure to avoid phrases like 'serial killer'."

"It's not my first rodeo," Liam said.

"Sorry," Mark said with a grimace. "Ladies, officers are going to be escorting you to your homes now. Plan on staying home for the next two or three days until we get this sorted out."

Jeremiah shook his head. Cooping kids up on winter break sounded like a recipe for disaster. Still, it was for their own safety.

Jeremiah stood up and walked over to Brenda and Sarah.

Sarah looked up at him. "I've already talked to my parents and Brenda and I are going to have a slumber party at her house for the next couple days."

Jeremiah was relieved to hear it. He knew the two girls would stick together like glue and watch out for each other. He fished a card out of his wallet.

"This has my cell phone number on it. It is not to be shared, but please use this if you want to talk to me," he said.

Brenda took the card from him with a grateful nod.

"Shouldn't all the Rabbi's Rangers have your number?" Sarah asked.

Jeremiah hesitated for a moment. He avoided giving out his private number whenever possible. In the case of the Rangers, though, every one of them deserved to have it. More than that, because of the connection they all shared he'd hate it if something ever happened to one of them and they needed him but couldn't reach him.

"Yes, but tell them this is Rangers only," he instructed.

"Rangers only," both Sarah and Brenda repeated.

He felt an unexpected swell of emotion and turned abruptly away. He came face to face with Candace who was regarding him with intense curiosity.

"Who are Rabbi's Rangers?" she asked.

"They are," he said shortly, indicating Sarah and Brenda. There was no way he was going to try and explain it to an outsider.

"Okay," Candace said, clearly deciding to let it go. "Are you sure I need police protection?"

"I'm sure it's a good idea whether you end up needing it or not," he said.

"Alright. They seem to trust you. I will, too."

"Thank you, Candace," he said.

"What about the Escape! Channel people?" Becca asked.

Jeremiah had forgotten for a moment about Kyle and Bunni and the rest.

"They're wrapping up filming for the day," Josh said. "I told them they can have the park early tomorrow morning. They should be able to get more done then when there aren't any players around gawking."

"I'll assign a couple of officers to be here with them," Mark said.

It would also allow them to keep a closer eye on the crew Jeremiah realized. Hopefully it wasn't needed.

~

Cindy, Geanie, and Joseph kept going over what little they knew or could guess about the secret society. Cindy felt terrible, though, because her mind kept drifting back to

The Zone and she wished she knew what was happening there. When her phone rang she jumped.

"Hello?" she said, eager to hear Jeremiah's voice.

"Mark and I are heading back," Jeremiah told her. "How are things there?"

"A bit tense," she admitted.

"Well, hold tight. We'll get there as quick as we can."

Jeremiah arrived a short while later and she met him in the entryway and hugged him tight. They held onto each other for a minute, both relieved that Brenda hadn't been the girl killed but both worried that she was in danger.

They were still holding each other when Mark came in the door.

"How did you get here before me?" Mark asked bluntly. "I know you walked those two girls to their cars. You had to have left ten minutes after I did."

"I drove fast, took shortcuts, and avoided all the speed traps. Didn't you do the same?" Jeremiah asked nonchalantly.

"How fast? No, don't tell me. I don't want to know." Mark shifted his focus to Cindy. "Where is Traci?"

"She went upstairs to lie down as soon as we got here. Lizzie went upstairs after her."

"Thanks. I'll be back down in a bit," Mark said, making a beeline for the stairs.

Cindy and Jeremiah walked into the living room where Joseph and Geanie were.

"How are you?" Joseph asked.

"In need of a vacation. A very long one," Jeremiah admitted.

"After this I think we'll all be," Joseph muttered.

"Didn't you say something about a dog show back east?" Jeremiah asked.

"Yup, end of February at the Zone World sports complex. It's going to be Clarice's last show before she retires."

"That sounds nice and relaxing," Jeremiah said.

Joseph chuckled. "Clearly you've never been to a dog show."

Captain padded into the room and nuzzled Jeremiah's hand as if on cue. Jeremiah crouched down and hugged the big dog. "What are you doing here?" he asked.

"I didn't know how long everyone was going to be so I took a drive and got Captain," Joseph said.

"What you say, Cap? You think you could win at a dog show?"

"He has good lines, but you don't know anything about his parentage, right?" Joseph asked.

Jeremiah smiled and shook his head. "Don't worry, Joseph, we're not going to try and give you and Clarice a run for best in show."

"Like you could," Joseph said. "When Clarice is around no one else stands a chance."

"Is she planning on having more puppies?" Jeremiah asked.

"Well, she hasn't given her two cents yet, but it is being discussed," Joseph said. "To be perfectly frank, I've been hesitant since what happened the last time there was a litter of puppies here."

"I don't think you have to worry about what happened last time happening this time," Cindy said.

"Of course not. Captain here will be the godfather and he'll stand watch to make sure no one comes near them," Jeremiah said.

Cindy couldn't help but smile at the image of the dog standing guard.

"Be careful, we just might take him up on that," Geanie said with a wan smile.

Jeremiah stood up and Captain scampered off. He took a seat on one of the sofas and looked around. "So, what did I miss?"

Cindy sat down next to him. "We're trying to figure out what we know about the secret society so we can take them down and keep Geanie safe."

"One thing I'd like to know is why are they targeting you now?" Jeremiah asked.

"Because of Ivan and the whole sting operation," Joseph said.

Jeremiah shook his head. "I get that, but if this organization is really made up of powerful, connected men, then why have they never approached you before that? In fact, why recruit Kenneth and Ivan? They wouldn't have fit the profile in my mind."

"Those are good questions," Joseph said. "As for Kenneth and Ivan, they were up-and-comers with a lot of ambition. I don't know much about Ivan but Kenneth was on the brink of marrying into a very prosperous family and taking the reins of the business. As to why they never approached me before, I don't know. Maybe no one ever thought I would go along with it before. For all I know people have tried to feel me out before like Ivan did and decided not to pursue. Or maybe they're doing a membership drive this year."

Any of those could be true, Cindy supposed. It would make a lot of sense that anyone who spoke with the real Joseph for five minutes would have concluded he was not a candidate. He'd been putting on an act for Ivan, trying to entice the other man into inviting him to join. Still, she could see why it was bothering Jeremiah.

"Do you still have that invitation they sent?"

"Mark has the original, but I have a picture," Joseph said.

He got out his phone, pulled it up and handed it to her. Even though she'd seen it before her blood still ran cold as she silently read it.

For the New Year we always choose three potential new members. Only one will have the skills, wit, and determination to do what has to be done. We cordially invite you to compete for that slot. To that end you have until midnight on New Year's Eve to kill your wife.

"It doesn't specifically threaten you or Geanie. What if you just ignore it?" she asked.

"Ivan killed himself before letting himself be caught. Something tells me these guys don't like loose ends. I'm not sure what that means for the two who fail, but I don't like it."

"Maybe we should be trying to figure out who the other two in the competition are," Geanie said.

Jeremiah shook his head. "They could be anyone literally anywhere in the country, maybe even the world. That would be like finding a needle in a haystack. Still, I'm sure Mark could do some digging and see if any wealthy wives have turned up dead lately."

"Just because they've told Joseph to kill his wife doesn't mean they'll all be wives. Ivan killed a stranger trying to get into the organization," Cindy pointed out.

"True, but it still doesn't hurt to check, particularly since we know Kenneth killed the girl he was sleeping with," Jeremiah said.

Cindy kept staring at the invitation. Something about it was really bothering her. She remembered it had been sent to Joseph here at the house.

"Weird," she said softly.

"What's that?" Joseph asked.

"Whoever sent this put a lot of money and effort into it. They couldn't risk it falling into the wrong hands. So, how did they know you'd be the one home to get it?" Cindy asked.

"They're watching him," Jeremiah said.

11

"That's just great!" Geanie blurted out, clearly distressed. "As if I wasn't already creeped out enough. Now you're telling me they're watching us?"

"It's going to be okay," Cindy said.

Jeremiah watched Joseph closely. The other man looked upset, but not surprised. He'd probably already guessed as much.

"Does this have anything to do with the bugs you found in the house months ago?" Joseph asked.

"I think those had more to do with me than you," Jeremiah said, shaking his head. "Besides, I disabled them. They couldn't be actively using those."

Joseph nodded.

"How are we supposed to beat them if we don't know how they're keeping tabs on us?" Geanie asked.

"I'll work on that angle," Jeremiah said.

"And we won't stop until we figure this out," Cindy added.

"There's one thing I can do," Joseph said.

"What's that?" Jeremiah asked.

"I can make some discreet inquiries about this group, see who's heard of them."

"I thought the whole point of a secret society is that it's secret," Cindy said.

"Yes, but rumors about these things almost always exist, especially among certain groups," Joseph said.

"It's true," Jeremiah nodded. "There's an old saying that the only way for two to keep a secret is if one is dead. Rumors, whispers always come out. Someone bragging here, a drunken comment there."

"Exactly!" Joseph said. "It does strike me as odd that I haven't heard about them and that they haven't tried to recruit me before if they are as all-powerful as everyone's making them out to be."

Jeremiah heard familiar footsteps outside the room.

"Mark's coming in," he said.

"How did you know that?" Mark asked a moment later as he appeared in the doorway.

"Heard you walking," Jeremiah said.

"It could have been Traci or Lizzie," he said.

Jeremiah didn't bother pointing out that he could recognize Mark by the length and rhythm of his stride and how heavily he stepped. He just shrugged instead.

"Are we solving the problems of the universe?" Mark asked as he sank into a chair.

"Attempting to," Cindy told him.

"Great. While we're at it I've got two to add."

"Which two?" Jeremiah asked.

"Figure out why someone would want to kill a cotton candy girl at The Zone and stop them is the first."

"And the second?" Cindy asked.

"Figure out how to help my wife," Mark said, his voice dropping to barely more than a whisper.

Cindy's face filled with compassion. Jeremiah knew that Cindy knew all too well what Traci was going through. For a time Cindy had even been plagued with PTSD.

Although that was something that could rear its head again at any time, he was grateful that it had been a long while since she'd actively struggled with it.

"She's going to be okay," Cindy said softly. "She just needs time and support and love."

"I hope so," Mark muttered. "I don't want to have to take the twins to visit their mom in a hospital."

Jeremiah straightened. He knew Traci was in bad shape, but hearing Mark say something like that surprised and worried him.

"Mark, everyone deals with grief, shock, and trauma in different ways," Jeremiah said. "How she deals with it in this case I don't think is as important as that she does deal with it and keeps moving forward. If she gets stuck that is when we should worry."

"Sufficient unto the day is the evil thereof," Cindy said.

"What?" Mark asked, looking puzzled.

Cindy cleared her throat. "As you know I used to be a lot more stressed about the world and the dangers in it. People used to quote Matthew six to me. That's the last part of the last verse in that chapter. It means that we shouldn't worry about tomorrow. I know that's a *lot* easier said than done. But I think you have to assume that Traci's going to get through this and not fill your head with doubts and fears and what ifs."

"She's right," Geanie said. "And it's good advice. For all of us," she said, staring directly at Joseph.

Joseph nodded solemnly.

Again, like he had with Christmas, Jeremiah felt slightly left out. He was aware that Matthew was one of the four gospels in the Christian New Testament, but that was all.

"Okay, I'll try to cool it with the premature stressing," Mark said.

"Good. Now, let's get busy with the problem that we can solve tonight. Let's figure out the cotton candy killer problem," Cindy said.

"Solve it tonight? You're optimistic," Mark said, clearly struggling to hold back a laugh.

"There's only so many possible motives for something like this," Cindy said. She counted them off on her fingers. "One, serial killer. Two, revenge."

"What, a disgruntled former cotton candy operator?" Mark asked. "I think they'd take their issues out on something or someone else other than the girls stuck at the same job."

"It could be someone wanting to hurt the park or its owners," Geanie said.

"Or someone wanting to extort money from them," Joseph said.

"Which brings us to three, some kind of horrible, twisted ransom scheme," Cindy said.

"Or what we were speculating on a little while ago, that one of the girls saw something she shouldn't have and a killer is trying to silence her," Mark said.

"And that was number four," Cindy said. "Great job."

"Gee, thanks," Mark said sarcastically. "Any other numbers you want to share?"

"Nope, just the four," Cindy said.

"Okay, then let's focus on number four. A couple of the girls saw people behaving a bit oddly, but not enough to really grab their attention. They couldn't even really give physical descriptions of the people. So, what would make someone so paranoid about being overheard or seen that they'd kill every girl who wore the uniform just to be sure they got the right one?" Mark asked.

"Let me try this one," Jeremiah said, giving Cindy a faint smile. He started holding up his fingers like she had. "One, criminal activity, buying or selling something. Two, terrorism. Three, compromising conversations that could cost careers, fortunes, or marriages."

"I'm hoping there's a fourth coming," Mark said, "because none of these is really working for me at the moment."

"And four, espionage."

A sudden chill danced up Jeremiah's spine. *And I know for a fact that a C.I.A. agent is in town and has an interest in the park.*

He didn't want to think that Martin could have anything to do with the murders of the two girls. He wasn't naïve enough, though, to believe that it was beyond the other man. If one of the girls had heard the wrong thing it might have put the agent between a rock and a hard place.

Jeremiah shook his head, dismissing the notion. If Martin had been behind it, he wouldn't have been so sloppy. He would have known or found out for sure which girl it was and wouldn't have just targeted any girl wearing the uniform.

"Okay, I like that idea even less," Mark growled.

"Fine, we can toss that one out," Jeremiah said. He hadn't told the others that Martin was in town. Now he was wondering if he should. Ultimately, he decided against it. He didn't know why Martin was in the area, but he did know that whatever was going on he didn't want Cindy and the others mixed up in it.

"So, what could one of the girls have seen or heard that someone was willing to keep private?" Mark asked.

"I lean more toward the idea that they might have heard something. If it was visible, someone exchanging something, I think the girls would have been more likely to notice," Jeremiah said.

"Plus, security checks everyone's bags," Geanie said. "So unless they worked there, I don't see anyone being able to smuggle in money or guns or drugs or anything like that."

"The first girl was killed in your backyard," Cindy said to Mark.

"Thanks for reminding me," he said.

"And it was close to her home, right?"

"Right."

"Then we might be looking at someone who works there. If they didn't, whoever it was would have had to follow the girl to find out where she lived. In which case there had to be better times or places to grab her. On the other hand, if it's someone who works at the park they could get into the computers and pull up her employee record and find her home address. They might have surprised her there, but she ran."

"She didn't run far enough," Mark said grimly.

"Regardless of whether or not the killer or an associate of his works at the park, there's desperation in this. You don't kill two people this close together unless you really need to silence someone in a hurry," Jeremiah said.

"Meaning what?" Cindy asked, almost as though she was reading his mind.

"I think whatever was overheard or seen had to have happened two days ago. This is rushed, sloppy work." Jeremiah said.

"So, you think if we can figure out which girls were working a couple of days ago, we can narrow down which one of them is the actual target?" Mark asked.

"I think we can narrow down which one might be the one who saw or heard something. I still think all the girls are in danger since the killer doesn't know which one he's looking for."

Mark pulled out his phone. "I've got Josh's number. Hopefully he can help us narrow this down."

The detective left the room while he placed the call. He was back shortly.

"He's getting it to me as fast as he can," Mark said.

"Josh Hanson?" Joseph asked.

"Yes. The son of the park's owners," Mark said. "Why, do you know him?"

Joseph nodded. "I haven't seen him in a couple of years, but I know the family."

"How well do you know them?" Mark asked.

"Well enough to be more than acquaintances. Not well enough to be actual friends," Joseph said.

Jeremiah couldn't help but wonder for a moment if Mr. Hanson was one of the people Joseph intended to mention the secret society to. A quarterback turned theme park mogul seemed like a likely candidate to capture the attention of the society.

~

Cindy was getting frustrated. It felt like they were going around in circles. They just didn't have enough to go on. She kept wondering how long before Josh called Mark back and let him know which girls had been working on the days in question.

The doorbell rang, startling everyone. She looked around the room at all the tense faces. There was this momentary sense of dread, like no one wanted to go see what bad news might have just shown up. Joseph's house didn't get many random visitors or salespeople. Whoever was at the door was there intentionally.

"I'll get it," Joseph finally said, voice strained. She had a feeling that he was half expecting to get another one of those terrible invitations or something just as disturbing from the secret society that expected him to kill Geanie.

He left the room and she stood, driven to go with him and find out for herself who was there. She had a flashback to when Keenan and several police officers stormed the place and arrested Jeremiah. The knot in her stomach only twisted more and she found that she was holding her breath as she stood in the foyer a safe distance from the door and watched Joseph open it.

A moment later Joseph stepped back. Someone was coming inside and the sickness inside doubled.

Josh and Candace from The Zone stepped inside and Cindy found herself sagging in relief. Josh shook hands with Joseph, then introduced Candace who also shook hands with Joseph.

"Hello," Cindy said with a little wave. "I didn't expect to see you again."

Josh held up a large envelope.

"I've got some information for the detective," Josh said. "I'm hoping it helps solve these murders."

He's being so helpful. That would be a clever tactic if he was the killer, she thought. Of course, there was no reason to suspect him and he seemed nice enough, but at the moment she wasn't entirely trusting of anyone except her little circle.

"Come in," Joseph said.

"How did you know he was here?" Cindy asked.

"He said this is where he'd be," Josh explained.

Cindy nodded and led them to the living room. Mark looked as surprised to see Josh and Candace as Cindy had been.

Josh handed him a large envelope.

"I hope this helps. It's a list of all the referees who were working the last three days. Yesterday, Theresa, Brenda, and Joy were working. Brie was supposed to, but she never showed or called in. Now we know why."

"Who was working on Christmas?" Mark asked.

"No one. The park is closed for Christmas Day."

Mark looked at him sharply. "Brie was wearing her uniform when her body was found early yesterday morning."

"I don't know what to tell you," Josh said. "Maybe she had an early morning, something to get to before work. There's no reason that I can think of why she'd have been wearing it the night before."

That certainly changed things some. It meant that whatever had triggered all this must have happened on Christmas Eve or earlier, Cindy realized.

"I also put all the footage from our surveillance cameras for Christmas Eve, yesterday, and today on a thumb drive in there. Hopefully it will help," Josh said.

"I'm sure it will. Thank you," Mark said.

"Can we get you anything to drink or cookies perhaps?" Geanie asked.

Josh shook his head. "We should be on our way. Thanks."

He and Candace turned to leave.

Mark's phone rang and he answered.

"What? I can't hear you," Mark said. "You're really faint."

Finally, Mark put his phone on speaker. Cindy recognized Liam's voice as soon as the other man began to talk.

"Shots fired at the home of one of the girls under surveillance," Liam said over the sound of a siren.

"Which one?" Mark asked.

"Brenda."

"Sarah's there with her," Jeremiah said as he jumped to his feet.

12

"Where do you think you're going?" Jeremiah heard Mark shout.

Jeremiah had pushed past Josh and Candace. He was already in the foyer and a second later he would be outside. "To help my Rangers," he said, not caring if the others took his meaning.

He made it outside and got in his car. As he put the key in the ignition Cindy opened the passenger door and got in.

"What are you doing?" he asked.

"I'm coming with you," she said.

"No, you need to stay here."

"Do you even know where Brenda lives?" she asked.

Jeremiah grimaced. He didn't.

"I suppose you do?" he asked.

"Yes."

"Give me the address."

"I'll do better. I'll give you directions."

Cindy put on her seatbelt and he instinctively felt that was the end of the discussion.

He started the car and headed down the hill. "I don't want to put you in danger," he said.

"At the moment you should be more worried about those girls than me."

She was right and he knew it. By the time they could get there, whatever was happening would be over. He just prayed the girls were safe.

~

"What can we do to help?" Josh asked.

"Nothing. Go home," Mark said shortly.

"Please," Candace said, eyes wide. "We need to do something. Zoners stick together."

Mark was about to tell them to go home again, a bit more forcefully this time, but he stopped short. Something in Candace's eyes reminded him of Cindy. The girl was determined to help, even if she was in way over her head.

"Have you looked at the security footage yet?" he asked as he pulled the thumb drive out of the envelope.

"No, we didn't have time to," Josh said.

"Well, get hold of a couple of laptops, make some copies, and start going through this looking for anything suspicious."

"I have laptops we can use," Joseph said.

"We can help go through the footage," Geanie said.

Josh shook his head. "It would be faster and easier for those of us who know the park to do it."

"I'm calling Becca," Candace said, pulling her phone out of her back pocket.

"Call Pete while you're at it. That man knows the park better than the rest of us," Josh said.

"On it."

Mark had the distinct feeling that he'd just lost control of the entire situation. It occurred to him to object, but honestly they were right that they'd be able to spot anomalies faster and would know at least some of the park employees on site.

"We'll set the laptops up in the dining room," Geanie said, getting up.

She swiftly exited the room, followed by Joseph.

As much as Mark wanted to go check on Brenda, he knew Liam, Jeremiah, and Cindy would handle things there. The best thing he could do was be here to help and take a look at anything the others found on the footage. And he'd be able to check in on Traci and if she woke up, he'd be there if she needed to talk.

"Only bring in people you trust absolutely," Mark said.

Josh and Candace both nodded.

"And make sure more than one person goes over the same footage."

"We can copy the drive and each of us will go over everything," Candace said.

"Our people are the ones in danger. We're here to see this through," Josh affirmed.

"Okay, then let's get this party started," Mark said.

~

Cindy's heart was pounding as Jeremiah drove like a maniac to get to Brenda's house. Even though it had been a couple of years, Cindy remembered crystal clear the rundown house on one of the worst streets in town. She would have been happier to hear that Brenda and Sarah were at Sarah's house instead.

When they got there several policemen were out front. Liam was one of them. Cindy got out of the car and made her way over to him.

"Are the girls alright?" she asked breathlessly.

"Shaken, but fine," Liam said.

"Did the killer come after Brenda?" Jeremiah asked as he came up behind Cindy.

"It's a bit more complicated than that," Liam said grimly.

"What do you mean?" Cindy asked.

"It appears that the shots came from a gun the family owned and that a family member fired. Whether it was an accident while cleaning it or a domestic disturbance isn't entirely clear."

Cindy's heart ached for Brenda. The poor girl had already been through so much.

"Can we see Brenda and Sarah?" Jeremiah asked.

"I'll bring them over here," Liam said.

He walked off and a minute later returned with both girls. They were shaken looking but seemed to be holding up far better than Cindy could have imagined. Both of them ran forward and hugged Jeremiah tight.

"Are you both okay?" Jeremiah asked.

His accent which most of the time was barely noticeable was thick. Cindy could tell just how worried he was about Brenda and Sarah by that alone. She wrapped her arms around all three of them.

"Rangers like group hugs," Brenda said in a quiet voice.

"We're okay," Sarah added. "We're going to my house once the policemen tell us we can go."

"That sounds like a good idea," Cindy said.

"We'll wait with you and then make sure you get over there okay," Jeremiah said.

"Thank you," both girls chorused.

Their relief was obvious. Being around Jeremiah made them feel safer. That was something Cindy could relate to.

~

Mark felt like he was going to start climbing the walls. Josh, Candace, Becca, and an older guy named Pete were all in the dining room, eyes glued to laptops as they went through security footage. Meanwhile he was keeping Pete supplied with coffee and Josh and Candace supplied with soda.

"Are you sure you don't want a soda?" he asked Becca as he brought a couple more Cokes into the room.

"No!" Josh, Candace, and Pete all shouted at the same time.

"Nothing with sugar for Becca," Josh said emphatically.

"This house is too nice for that," Pete said.

"I don't understand," Mark said.

"She's allergic to sugar," Josh explained. "It makes her a bit-"

"Crazy," Pete interjected.

"Hyper," Josh finished.

"It's true," Becca said with a sad little sigh.

"Out of her ever loving mind," Pete said.

"Okay, so no sugar for Becca," Mark said warily.

He went back to the kitchen wondering what on earth he had gotten himself into. *And I thought working with Jeremiah and Cindy was weird.*

"Any progress?" Joseph asked.

"I honestly wish I knew," Mark said as he sat down on one of the stools at the counter.

Joseph was up to his elbows in red sauce and was dipping tortillas into it.

"What are you making?" Mark asked as his stomach rumbled angrily.

"Enchiladas," Joseph said.

It was a testament to how weird the day had been that it was nearly ten o'clock at night and none of them had eaten dinner yet. He was grateful that Joseph was taking on the task of getting them all fed.

"Sounds good. I could eat my weight in them right about now," Mark said.

Joseph raised an eyebrow. "If you do then you have to go to the store to get more tortillas for the rest of us."

"Fine, I can share," Mark said, enjoying the gentle banter. "Where'd your better half scamper off to?"

"She's upstairs checking to see if Traci and Lizzie want to come down for dinner. She's also checking guest rooms just in case we end up with unexpected overnight guests."

Mark couldn't help but chuckle. "I think you guys are happiest when the house is full of people."

Joseph shrugged as he kept working.

"What can I say? We enjoy entertaining," he said.

"And you do it so well."

"Thank you," Joseph said.

"Sorry to interrupt," a soft voice said.

Mark turned to see Lizzie hovering just inside the kitchen, looking uncertain.

"Lizzie, you're not interrupting. Come in," Mark said, forcing a smile across his face. The truth was of all Traci's family, Lizzie was the one he'd had the least contact with and most of that had been negative. It was clear that she had changed a lot since her experiences with the coven and

119

he was doing his best to be welcoming. He was sure she had people waiting in line to judge her and he didn't need to add to it.

"Thank you," she said.

She came in and sat down on one of the stools.

"You're just in time. I've been making enchiladas and the first batch is almost ready," Joseph said cheerfully.

"And since we're the only ones who know that, we get first crack at them," Mark said jovially. "The others can fend for themselves."

"Mark, is that nice?" Joseph chided gently.

"It might not be nice, but it is nature. Survival of the hungriest."

Lizzie smiled at that while Joseph chuckled.

"Is Traci awake?" Mark asked.

"Yes," Lizzie said with a nod. "She said she'd like to eat in the room."

"That's fine. We have no shortage of bed trays here," Joseph said.

"You don't have a shortage of anything here," Mark said sarcastically.

"Want not, waste not," Joseph said with an air of innocence.

Lizzie frowned.

"That's not how that goes," Mark said.

"Really? Odd," Joseph said.

Mark rolled his eyes.

~

"You know what I just thought about?" Cindy said.

"What?" Jeremiah asked.

He fought the urge to glance over at her. Instead he kept his eyes fixed on the road and Sarah's car in front of them. Sarah and Brenda were heading for Sarah's house and Cindy and he were following as he had promised they would.

"Next year at this time we'll be on our honeymoon."

"That can't come too soon," he said.

She laughed at that.

"What?" he asked.

"While I agree with you in theory, we have a lot to do to get ready for the wedding."

"What's next on our checklist?" he asked.

"We need to send out save the date announcements."

"Why don't we just send out invitations?" he asked.

"Because you don't send those out until closer."

"Why?" he asked.

"Because..." Cindy hesitated. "You know, I'm not sure. I guess closer to the date people can more firmly commit to whether they're going and bringing a guest or not."

"Okay. Can we just put save the date announcements in bulletins for the synagogue and church? I mean, I assume we're inviting everyone from both."

"Yes, I think that would work," Cindy said. There was something slightly off in her voice that he caught.

"What's wrong?" he asked.

"I know our engagement is public knowledge, I'm just wondering if things are going to get more intense once the date is announced and everything. I'm wondering how many from my church and your synagogue are going to even come."

So far she had caught a lot more flak than he had. He wished she hadn't, but it was what it was.

"Those two girls in the car in front of us will be there," he said softly. "One from my synagogue and one from your church."

"You're right," Cindy said. "You know it really is amazing how close those girls, really that whole group of kids, has remained."

"They had to take care of each other while people were stalking and trying to kill them. That creates a pretty strong bond," he said.

"We wouldn't know anything about that," she said. Her tone was lighter now and he could tell that she was smiling.

He reached over and grabbed her hand. "No, we wouldn't know anything about that," he agreed.

A few seconds later the car they were following slowed and turned into a driveway. Jeremiah stopped and watched as both girls got out of the car. They grabbed some stuff from the backseat then went up to the front door. Sarah unlocked it and then they both turned to wave before disappearing inside.

The door closed and Jeremiah relaxed slightly.

"They should be safe here," Cindy said.

Jeremiah nodded. She was right, but he wasn't going to feel better until the killer was caught.

"Okay, let's go check back in with the others," he said.

As he drove away he had a sudden urge to turn and go back. He almost did, but decided against it. There was a difference between cautious and paranoid and he was pretty sure he had crossed the line.

They're safe, he thought.

He just wished he believed himself.

~

Mark's phone buzzed and he checked it.

"Looks like Cindy and Jeremiah are heading back. Cindy says the girls are okay."

"That's a relief," Joseph said. "Although I'm going to have to feed them something. I'm sure they haven't eaten."

"Oh darn, you're going to have to make more enchiladas," Mark said. "And if a couple of them happen to make it into my stomach, well, I'll just have to live with it."

"Mark, do we need to discuss stress eating?"

"I've got to keep up my energy. You should want that for me."

"You've already had enough enchiladas to keep a small army going."

"Speaking of small armies, you'll probably want to make extra for Jeremiah. We definitely need him to keep his strength up."

"Detective!" someone shouted from the dining room.

Mark hopped off the kitchen stool and headed to the other room. When he made it there Josh waved him over.

"Did you find something in the surveillance footage?" Mark asked.

"Not yet," Josh said, his voice tense.

"Then what is it?"

"There are fan websites and forums online dedicated to The Zone parks. People give travel tips, rate restaurants, that kind of thing," Josh said.

"Okay, yeah. So why is that important?"

"Because on one of them someone posted this."

He sat back from his screen and Mark leaned in to see what he was looking at.

There was a blurry picture of a girl wearing a white and pink striped shirt heading away from the camera. The picture only captured her from the shoulders down and it was impossible to tell what color hair she had. It could easily have been any of the girls he'd spoken to that day. He wasn't sure why the picture was significant until he realized that whoever had posted it included a caption.

A chill went down Mark's spine as he stared at what was written.

Help me find the one that got away!

13

"This is the girl the killer is trying to find," Josh said, voice tight.

"How did you come across this?" Mark asked.

"I was taking a five-minute break from the security footage, just trying to rest my brain. I decided to check out the most popular websites and see if anyone was talking about the park closure today or what happened. This was posted four hours ago. Whoever did it is making out that he met her and neglected to get her name and is trying to find her."

"Have there been any responses?" Mark asked.

"Several. This one is particularly concerning, though," Josh said, scrolling down and then pointing to one user comment.

"I know all the cotton candy girls, but I'm not sure they'd appreciate having their names given out online to a stranger. If you like her that much, go back to the park and look for her," Mark read out loud. "It's posted by a guy named Mascot Kurt."

"Kurt?" Candace asked, sounding surprised.

"Yeah, you know him?" Mark asked.

Candace blushed fiercely. "He's my ex-boyfriend," she said quietly.

"He works at the park as a mascot, a costumed character," Josh said. "He posts a lot in these forums and he's not all that careful. It wouldn't be too hard for someone to find him."

"And get some names out of him," Mark muttered.

"Lisa," Candace said.

"Excuse me?" Mark said.

"Lisa, one of the cotton candy operators. She's dating him."

"This guy just really has a thing for cotton candy, doesn't he?" Mark asked.

Candace blushed again.

"Do you know where he lives?" Mark asked.

Josh nodded. "I can give you the address."

He pulled out his phone, pulled up a contact, and handed it to Mark.

"You have your girlfriend's ex-boyfriend's address?" Mark asked.

"Yeah. I had to pick her up from a party there last year," Josh said.

Mark was impressed at the fact that Josh didn't seem the least bit ruffled or even jealous. Either he was the most relaxed, understanding guy or he was a gifted actor.

"I still have his phone number," Candace said.

"Text me the number and a picture if you have one," Mark said. "I'll try calling on my way over there."

Mark texted Liam Kurt's address and asked him to meet him there. The text from Candace came in and Mark nodded. He left the house, got in his car, and called as he started down the hill. It rang and then went to voicemail.

"Kurt, this is Detective Mark Walters with the Pine Springs Police Department. Candace gave me your number. I'm hoping you can help us with an ongoing investigation. It is urgent that you call me back at this number as soon as you get this message."

Mark ended the call and focused on the road ahead of him. The kid might be away from his phone or screening calls. He should have called from Candace's phone since the guy probably would have been more likely to pick up if he thought she was calling. He hoped he hadn't spooked him too much with the message. Most people went a lifetime with very little contact with police officers and they could get edgy when they suddenly had to deal with them.

~

Something was still scratching at the back of Jeremiah's mind as he drove back to Joseph and Geanie's. He kept thinking he should have escorted Sarah and Brenda inside the house. There was no reason why the killer should be looking for Brenda there. Still, it was bothering him.

"What is it?" Cindy asked.

She was getting better and better at sensing his moods. Sometimes it felt like she was almost reading his mind. He'd never been close enough with someone before to have them pick up on what he was thinking and feeling. It was nice, but for a man who had spent a lifetime hiding in shadows and behind masks it was also a bit disconcerting.

He thought about downplaying it, but decided that maybe sharing would help him get the worry out of his mind.

"It's going to sound paranoid, but I keep feeling like I should have walked the girls into the house," he said.

"Why didn't you?"

"I don't know. I thought they were safe. I guess I also didn't want to worry the girls or Sarah's parents any more than they already are. That probably doesn't make any sense."

"No, it does," Cindy said.

"I just need to let it go."

"Or we could go back and check on them," Cindy said.

"And that would probably really raise an alarm."

"Not if we are returning something one of the girls lost in the car," Cindy said.

"Did they leave something behind?" Jeremiah asked, risking a quick glance at the backseat.

"No, but we could ask them if this is their phone," Cindy said, pulling her own phone out of her purse. "Then when they say it isn't, we apologize for disturbing them and move along."

Jeremiah chuckled. "That's pretty devious."

"Maybe I should be a spy," Cindy said with a smirk.

"Maybe you should."

"What would my cool spy name be?" she asked.

"You want a cool spy name?"

He pulled into a left-hand turn lane so he could make a U-turn and head back to Sarah's house.

"Yes, all the coolest spies have great names or nicknames. I want one, too."

"Let me think," Jeremiah said.

He loved this playful side of her so much. He had been given a nickname by those in the business. It was a dark name and one he had been trying to shake with no real luck. He had been known as the Angel of Death. Even though he was no longer an assassin, it felt like he still killed his share of people every few months.

He didn't do it because he wanted to, but because it was necessary. He thought about one of the things his former handler had once told him. *We do the dark deeds that need to be done because no one else can.*

He was still doing those dark deeds. Maybe that was because there would always be dark deeds that required someone willing to do them.

"Earth to Jeremiah," Cindy said, interrupting his thoughts.

"What?"

"Light is green."

Jeremiah made the U-turn and started back toward Sarah's.

"Does it take that much thought to come up with my spy name?" Cindy asked.

"Sorry." He took a deep breath. "Angel of Mercy."

"That doesn't sound much like a spy," she said.

She was right. It didn't. What it did sound like was his exact opposite. That was fitting because in so very many ways she was. He marveled, as he often did, at the crazy paths their lives had taken in order to bring them together.

"I love you," he said.

"I love you, too."

"Okay, so you want a better spy name. Cinderblock."

"Excuse me?" she said.

"It's Cindy turned into cinder and a cinderblock because it's unyielding, strong, just like you."

There was a long pause and then he saw her shake her head.

"That's it. You officially do *not* get to name our children."

"Don't be so dismissive. The stone the builders rejected has become the cornerstone."

"Jeremiah!" she blurted out, so loudly he jerked slightly.

"What?" he asked, wondering what she'd seen on the road that he'd missed.

"You just quoted Jesus," she said.

"Um, no. I quoted the Psalmist."

"Matthew 21:42," she said.

"Psalm 118:22," he countered.

"Both! Jesus was quoting scripture," Cindy said.

"Does this mean that you're okay with being Cinderblock?" he asked.

It was a ridiculous question, but a sudden unease had seized him and he desperately wanted it to go away.

"No! I'm not okay with being Cinderblock," she said.

"Oh, I think that's your new name."

"What this does mean is something special, miraculous," she said.

"How do you figure?" he asked.

"I remembered the book, chapter, and verse."

"So?"

"I *never* remember the address of a verse I'm looking for. The only ones I know for sure are Genesis 1 and Psalm 23. I always have to look up where everything else is."

"You sure Matthew 21:42 is where Jesus quoted the Psalm?" he asked.

"One hundred percent. Isn't that unbelievable?"

If it was a miracle as she claimed, then he had to wonder what it meant. It was interesting that the verse she was quoting was one of the ones he knew by heart from the

Psalms. It was one of the scriptures he had read often when he was younger.

"Earth to Jeremiah. I seem to have lost you again," Cindy said.

"Sorry, just really easily distracted tonight."

"It's okay," she said, reaching out and squeezing his knee.

"And now you're trying to distract me more."

"Not intentionally."

"Whatever you say, Cinderblock."

She made a shrieking sound and hit his arm. He smiled. There was no way he was letting this go anytime soon. Especially when it caused her to make that sound. It was adorable.

A few minutes later they finally pulled up outside Sarah's house. Cindy handed Jeremiah her phone.

"It will look more casual if just one of us goes up to the door," she said.

She was right. He took the phone and got out of the car. The house looked dark. He couldn't see any lights from the street. He was pretty sure it had looked the same when he waved goodbye to the girls a few minutes earlier.

He strode carefully up the walk, not wanting to trip over anything in the dark. When he reached the front door he found the doorbell and rang it. He could hear it echoing inside.

A minute later a man in his forties opened the door and gazed at him quizzically.

"Can I help you?" he asked.

"Yes, hi. I'm Rabbi Silverman from the synagogue. You must be Sarah's father."

Jeremiah had seen Sarah with her mother at the synagogue many times, but hadn't yet met her father.

"Yes, I am. Rabbi, it's good to meet you. Sarah has told me so much about you," he said.

"She's a remarkable young woman. You've done a great job raising her."

"Thanks. It's mostly her mother, though. That woman puts everything she has into this family."

"Could I see Sarah for a minute?" Jeremiah asked.

"She told us that she and her friend Brenda were so worn out from the excitement earlier that they were going straight to her room and to sleep. If you want to come in, I can go and wake them up."

"No, that's alright," Jeremiah said. "I just wanted to make sure they were okay."

"I appreciate that. I'll tell her in the morning that you stopped by."

Jeremiah returned to his car and got in. He handed Cindy's phone back to her.

"Well?" she asked.

"Sarah's dad answered the door. He said the girls were worn out and went straight upstairs to bed."

"Given everything that makes sense," Cindy said.

"Maybe," Jeremiah said.

"What is it?"

How could Jeremiah explain to her that after a lifetime spent in the shadows you gained a sense of when things weren't quite right.

Or when someone isn't quite right.

He reached for his phone. He called Marie's cell. Unfortunately, the call went to voicemail. He left a message asking her if there was a directory photo or anything of Sarah's family, particularly her father.

"What now?" Cindy asked.

"We wait," he said tensely. Sometimes it was hard to be rabbi Jeremiah when assassin Jeremiah wanted nothing more than to storm the house and find out the truth.

~

Liam was waiting in the parking lot of Kurt's apartment building when Mark showed up.

"Rebecca made me dinner tonight. She's got it in the stove keeping it warm," Liam said by way of greeting.

Mark grunted. "She should get used to that. It comes with being a cop's wife."

"Fingers crossed," Liam said.

"You don't think she'll turn you down, do you?"

"I'm never quite sure what she's going to do," Liam said.

"Well, at least that keeps life interesting."

"That's one word."

"What's wrong with interesting?" Mark asked.

"It's the subject of a Chinese curse. May you live in interesting times."

"Yeah, well if you wanted peace and tranquility and all that other stuff you shouldn't have become a cop."

"I became a cop so other people could have those things," Liam said.

"Noble. A bit stupid maybe, but noble."

"And why did you become a cop?"

"To be honest, I don't think I remember anymore," Mark said, looking at a rickety looking flight of stairs. "This place doesn't have an elevator does it?"

"From the looks of it this place was built before that was a requirement," Liam said.

"Great."

"So, why are we here?" Liam asked.

"Someone went on a website and posted a picture of a cotton candy girl and said he was looking for her."

"You think the killer did that?"

"Maybe."

"That's a gutsy move," Liam said.

"That's one way of looking at it."

"Anyway, this guy Kurt admitted to knowing all of them but wouldn't give out their information."

"So, you think the killer would actually track him down looking for it?" Liam asked, skepticism in his voice.

"I know, it's a longshot, but it's all we got."

They made it upstairs and headed down the row of apartments until they found Kurt's. Mark knocked on the door and waited.

The door to the apartment next door opened and a woman stared out.

"You the police?" she asked.

"Yes, ma'am," Liam said.

"It's about time. It's been forever since I called in that complaint."

"Excuse me, ma'am, which complaint?" Mark asked quickly.

"About them, next door. I don't know what they have going on, but there was a whole lot of screaming," she said.

"Ma'am, we need you to get back inside," Liam said.

She closed the door and Mark looked at Liam.

"Someone screaming for help might be what she heard," he said.

"Works for me," Mark said.

Mark reached out and grabbed the doorknob. It was unlocked.

Liam pulled his gun as Mark pushed the door open. Liam moved quickly inside, through the main room and into the back.

Mark made it into the main room and stopped.

"Clear!" Liam shouted from the back before returning.

Mark stared at a body on the ground. The man was bloody and unmoving. It looked like someone had beaten the guy to death. Mark crouched down next to the body to get a closer look. Swollen and discolored as the face was, he still recognized it from the picture he had seen earlier.

It was Kurt.

14

"Is he dead?" Liam asked.

"He looks like it," Mark said.

He held his hand in front of Kurt's face. The tiniest bit of breath touched it.

"Call for an ambulance. He's alive."

Liam called it in. Then he crouched down next to Mark.

"Someone wanted something from this guy," Liam said.

Mark looked around the room. There was a blood-stained dining room chair with bloody ropes tied to the arms of it. Kurt's wrists were raw and swollen. Someone had tied him to the chair while they were beating him.

"Like the names of all the other girls in the park who sell cotton candy?" Mark asked.

"You think he gave them to the guy?"

"He's like what, nineteen? Twenty? And he works at The Zone. Do you honestly think he could stand up forever under torture?" Mark asked.

"Could you?" Liam asked.

"No. I'd like to think so, but I know that every man has a breaking point," Mark said. He couldn't help but remember the dark day when he had tortured the land developer who had sent the assassins to Green Pastures. Life had only got stranger since that day.

Liam put his hand on Mark's shoulder.

"You're a lot stronger than you think you are," Liam said softly.

"Maybe, but I'm not in any hurry to test that theory," Mark said.

A shiver went down his spine. Again he'd had that terrible, morbid thought. What if something happened to Traci and him? He wanted to be there to watch his kids grow up. He was going to teach them both to throw a baseball. He was going to cry when they graduated high school and again when they graduated college.

"You okay?" Liam asked.

"No," Mark said.

"Look. It's been a rough couple of days. Why don't you take off? I've got this," Liam said.

Mark didn't want to just ditch Liam, but the thought was incredibly appealing.

"You're sure?" he asked.

"Yeah," Liam said.

In the distance Mark could hear the wail of sirens. He nodded slowly and stood up.

"Thanks, man."

"It's okay. Give Traci my love."

"I will."

~

Cindy glanced over at Jeremiah. She could tell that he was worried. They'd been sitting outside Sarah's house for about twenty minutes. Marie had yet to call back.

"Do you want to go to the synagogue? There should be a directory in the office," she said.

Jeremiah shook his head, eyes still fixed on the house.

"Why don't you call the girls? Didn't you give them both your phone number?"

"That's right," Jeremiah said softly. He grabbed his phone and tried calling.

"Sarah's phone is going to voicemail," he said after several seconds.

"Which it would if she were asleep," Cindy pointed out.

"Hi, Sarah, it's Rabbi Silverman. Please give me a call the moment you get this. I just want to make sure you and Brenda are okay tonight."

He ended the call and in short order was leaving a similar message on Brenda's phone.

A bit of inspiration struck Cindy and she grabbed her own phone and called Mark.

"Everything okay with you two?" Mark asked in lieu of a greeting.

"Yeah. We're outside Sarah's house. We dropped her and Brenda off here earlier and something just doesn't seem quite right. Could you come by and talk to the dad? Hopefully he'll let you in to see the girls."

"He has to, they're part of an ongoing murder investigation and the one is a potential victim."

"Great. Can you just get over here and make that happen?"

There was a long pause. Finally, Mark answered.

"It can't wait?" he asked.

The fact that he asked that was testament to how tired he was. Cindy glanced at Jeremiah. His jaw was clenched, and he was staring fixedly at the house. If they didn't get the detective over there she was afraid Jeremiah was going to do something rather rash.

"No, it can't."

"Fine. Text me the address."

Mark hung up unceremoniously. Cindy quickly sent him the address like he'd requested then settled back in to wait.

The house still appeared dark. That seemed a bit odd to her given that they knew the dad was awake. Or, at least, he should be still.

"Was the dad wearing pajamas when he answered the door?" she asked.

"No, normal clothes. Including shoes," Jeremiah said.

She should have asked Mark where he was so she could determine how far away he was. It had sounded like he was in his car as opposed to Geanie and Joseph's house. Of course, that led her to wonder what he was doing out. Questions swirled in her mind, but they would have to wait until he got there.

"That was good thinking, calling Mark," Jeremiah said.

"Thanks. I just hope he can help set our minds at ease."

"Me, too."

~

Mark desperately wanted to call Traci. He needed to hear the sound of her voice. He didn't want to wake her, though. He didn't know whether she actually was sleeping, but he hoped she was. Stress like she had been feeling took a terrible toll on the body as well as the mind. She needed all the rest she could get. They both did, but he was pretty sure he wouldn't be getting rest anytime soon, particularly with Cindy and Jeremiah just adding on.

He couldn't blame them. After all, it wasn't their fault that people did crazy, terrible things. All his friends were really guilty of was a constant, irritating ability to be in the wrong place at the right time. Even then some would argue that the duo was always right where they needed to be to solve murders and save lives.

He called Geanie who sounded surprised when she answered the phone.

"Mark, is everything okay?" she asked.

"When is it ever?" he grumbled.

"What's wrong?"

"Nothing new. I'm going to be a little while longer and I was just wondering if you'd had eyes on Traci since she got back to your house earlier."

"No. Do you want me to go check on her?"

He hesitated for a moment. He didn't want to disturb her if she was resting, but he needed to know and he trusted Geanie's opinion.

"Yes, please."

"Okay, I'll call you back in a couple of minutes."

"Thanks."

He waited what felt like an eternity for her to call back. In reality it was only five minutes, but it might as well have been forever.

"How is she?" he asked, answering as soon as the phone rang.

"I've seen her better, but she doesn't seem as bad as she did earlier," Geanie said. "She did eat a little and she has color in her cheeks."

"That's good."

"I'm taking her back up some tea and I'm going to sit with her and pray with her for a while."

"Thank you," Mark said, unsure what else to say. He was still getting used to Traci fully participating in

Christian activities. He'd seen her pray before, and she'd even dragged him into it a time or two. It was still weird, though.

"Of course," Geanie said. "Is there anything you need."

"So many things. A vacation. Peace and quiet. A single holiday to pass without mayhem. And Traci to be her usual happy, laughing self."

"I can at least help with one of those things," Geanie said.

Mark was startled. He must have been more tired than he thought because he hadn't realized he had said all that out loud.

"Um, sorry. Just thinking out loud," he said.

"Don't apologize. Life has been a bit rough for a while for all of us. I think we've all eased into a perpetual state of expecting trouble."

There was a brooding sound to her voice that he didn't like. He couldn't have Geanie go down the dark path Traci was on.

"So, where are you sending me on vacation?" he asked, trying to put a teasing note into his voice.

"Where do you want to go?" she asked.

"Well, I figure there's not much going on in Antarctica, so I'm thinking we could get some serious peace and quiet there."

Geanie laughed which made him feel better.

"Something tells me you could even find trouble there."

"No, you're mistaking me for our mutual friends. I've actually been feeling sorry for the local police of wherever they end up honeymooning."

Geanie laughed even harder. "Can you imagine?"

"I have. Many times. It makes me shudder. Then it makes me laugh because I realize they'll be someone else's problem and not mine."

"You think that now, but just wait."

"For what?"

"You know the local police will be calling you because Jeremiah and Cindy will give you as a reference. Then you'll get to explain that no matter what weird situation they found themselves in the middle of they are not suspects and that it's better to work with them than try to shut them out."

"Why do they enjoy making my life so hard?" Mark asked.

"Yes, because it's all about you," she said sarcastically.

"You mean they torment other people besides me?"

Geanie laughed so hard she made a snorting sound.

"I'll take that as a 'yes'. Well, good to know. Misery loves company."

"You know the thing though?"

"What?" Mark asked.

"Without all the crazy, none of us might be where we are."

"You're right," he said.

He wouldn't trade the friendships he had made for the world. He felt a surge of emotion and tried to tamp it down. It was not the time to wax sentimental.

"Okay, I've got to go do some police work," he said.

"Be safe," she said.

"I will."

~

Jeremiah was hungry and he was getting impatient. Cindy was squirming uncomfortably in the passenger seat. Suddenly her stomach growled angrily and loudly, disrupting the silence in the car.

"Sorry," she muttered as Jeremiah smiled at her.

"Don't apologize," he said.

Headlights appeared down the street and moments later Mark parked his car by theirs. Jeremiah rolled down the window as Mark got out of his car and approached.

"You two okay?" Mark asked.

"I'm hungry," Cindy muttered.

"That's because you missed dinner. Joseph made enchiladas. They were delicious. Don't feel bad about missing it, though. I ate yours for you," Mark said with a smirk.

Jeremiah had a fleeting, unreasoning desire to slap the look off his face.

"Thou shalt not covet thy neighbor's enchiladas," Jeremiah said.

"Yeah, well, what can I say? They were worth it."

Cindy started giggling really hard like she did sometimes when she was tired. It was adorable.

"So, what is it you want me to do?" Mark asked.

"Go up to the house and tell the guy who answers the door that you have some follow up questions for Sarah and Brenda," Jeremiah said.

"Because there's something suspicious about him?" Mark asked.

"I don't know," Jeremiah admitted.

Mark raised an eyebrow and shook his head. He heaved a sigh. "Okay, I'll see what I can do."

Jeremiah watched as Mark walked up to the front door. He rang the bell and after a few seconds knocked loudly. There was no sign of light or movement in the house. Mark tried again and after a minute came back to the car.

"No one's answering. Of course, it is almost eleven o'clock and everyone could be asleep. I didn't hear a doorbell actually ring inside, so it might not be working or might be too quiet to wake people. We could try calling the girls."

"Already did," Jeremiah said.

"Is there anything more we can do?" Cindy asked.

Mark shook his head. "Without any reasonable, articulable suspicion I can't go in there guns blazing. No one heard a scream or saw anything weird, right?"

Jeremiah knew that Mark was giving them the opportunity to lie and say that they had. However, that could create problems for all three of them, particularly if there really was nothing amiss.

"No," Jeremiah said.

"Okay, without that I'd need to get a warrant to go in," Mark said. "I'm sorry."

"It's okay. You tried," Jeremiah said.

"Thank you," Cindy said.

"Okay. Race you back to Joseph and Geanie's," Mark said as he headed back to his car.

"I guess we're done here for the night," Jeremiah said, feeling frustrated.

"I'm sure they're fine. They'll wake up in the morning and call you back," Cindy said.

He sincerely hoped so.

Mark drove off and Jeremiah followed after a moment.

They drove in silence for a couple of minutes.

"Do you think there will be enchiladas?" Cindy asked finally.

"I hope so," he said fervently.

"Do you think we should pick up fast food just in case?"

"We could, but I'm pretty sure Joseph would have saved us some," Jeremiah said.

"I hope so," she muttered.

Mark hadn't been kidding about racing them back. The detective had been speeding and they'd lost him at the first intersection when he blew through a light that was just turning red. He was clearly anxious to get back to the house. He was probably worried about Traci.

They were almost at the turn for Joseph and Geanie's house when his cell rang. He glanced at it.

"It's Marie," Jeremiah said. "Can you answer it?"

He handed her the phone.

"Hi, Jeremiah's phone, this is Cindy speaking," she said.

There was a couple of moments of silence. He could hear Marie's voice, but couldn't make out what she was saying.

"Jeremiah, turn the car around. We have to go back!" Cindy exclaimed.

"What?" he asked.

"Sarah's father died six years ago."

15

Jeremiah made a U-turn in the middle of the street and slammed his foot down on the accelerator. The car jumped ahead.

He should have never hesitated, never doubted his own gut. He pictured the man who had opened the door. The guy had been good, calm, confident. Jeremiah was going to snap his neck if he'd done anything to hurt Sarah or Brenda.

"Should I call Mark or 911?" Cindy asked.

"Neither," Jeremiah said with a growl.

He wasn't waiting on anyone. Every second wasted in getting into that house put the girls in danger. Next to him Cindy had begun to pray out loud, desperate, frantic prayers for the girls' safety.

When he turned onto Sarah's street he turned off the headlights and slowed down. He parked three houses down and turned to Cindy.

"As soon as I'm gone, drive at least two blocks away and call Mark."

In case the murderer managed to slip past him he didn't want to make Cindy a tempting target either for carjacking or hostage taking.

"No way," she said, shaking her head fiercely.

"I'm not asking," he growled.

She turned pale but she stared back at him, unblinking.

He forced himself to take a deep breath. "It's important," he said.

He could tell she was prepared to stand her ground and argue, but she glanced at the house and nodded. She knew as well as he that every second they debated the issue was potentially deadly for the girls they were there to save.

"Okay. Be careful. And call me the first moment you can."

"I promise," he said.

He swiftly kissed her then got out of the car.

He hesitated for a moment and then she got out and ran around to the driver's seat. He nodded at her and she started the car back down the road. Fortunately, she left the headlights off. He didn't want anything alerting the guy to their presence.

~

Mark noticed that Jeremiah hadn't taken him seriously about racing back to the house. It was just as well. Not only was he certain that he would have lost that race, but he was also pretty sure that two cars racing through Pine Springs would not have gone unnoticed, particularly if one of them was discovered to belong to a cop.

Joseph greeted him at the front door with a small pack of dogs. Buster was particularly excited to see Mark.

"Everyone's a little too keyed up to sleep," Joseph said. "I think they're hoping Santa Claus is coming again tonight."

"Wouldn't that be nice?" Mark asked as he bent down to rub the beagle's belly. "Where's everyone?"

"Geanie is still upstairs with Traci and Lizzie. The others are in the dining room where you left them."

Mark nodded. As much as he wanted to go upstairs and wrap his arms around Traci and leave them there for the next few hours, he had some business to attend to first.

"Have they found anything else?" Mark asked.

"Not yet, I don't think," Joseph said. "I keep running caffeine in to them and checking up every fifteen minutes or so."

"That's a lot of caffeine," Mark noted, vaguely impressed.

He stood up and Buster and the other dogs went running off. Mark followed Joseph to the dining room. There he stood in the doorway for a minute observing the group inside. They were all hunched over their laptops in a way that made his shoulders ache just watching them.

Becca, in particular, was scowling hard at her screen.

"You know, this would go a lot faster if I could just have some Christmas cookies," Becca said.

"No!" the others in the room chorused.

"Come on," Becca said. "I could fast forward through all the footage and find what we're looking for in no time."

"No one needs that," Josh said.

"Besides, this is a nice place. I wouldn't want to see it get all busted up," Pete said.

Mark exchanged a quick look with Joseph. He could tell the other man was wondering just how bad Becca really was with sugar. Her friends and coworkers made it sound like her getting her hands on some would be catastrophic. It was hard to believe that an allergy to sugar could make someone that crazy.

Becca hopped up from her chair and everyone around the table jumped.

"Becca, what are you doing?" Candace asked.

"Relax. I'm just stretching," Becca said.

She started walking around the table, shaking out her hands and wrists. Mark was quick to note that everyone else hit pause on their videos and just sat, watching her warily.

Becca paused behind Josh and he twisted in his seat to look at her. She was staring into space with a frown on her face.

"What is it?" Josh asked.

"Let me see that photo again, the one the creepy guy posted," Becca said.

"Sure," Josh said, turning back to his computer screen.

He pulled the picture from the website up and Mark stepped forward, anxious to know why Becca was wanting to see the picture.

Becca, leaned down, squinting at the slightly blurry picture of the cotton candy vendor that the killer was trying to find.

"Can you make it bigger and zoom in on the shoes?" she asked.

Josh did and Mark could see that the cotton candy vendor was wearing white tennis shoes with pink and white striped shoelaces. A bell went off in the back of his mind and he was sure that he had seen those shoelaces earlier that day.

"I know who it is," Becca said.

"How?" Joseph asked.

"We did Secret Santa among the referees this year. I bought those shoelaces for my person."

"Who is it?" Mark asked.

"Brenda."

As Mark reached for his phone it began to ring.

~

"Mark! That wasn't Sarah's father! We think the girls are in trouble and Jeremiah has gone in to try and help them," Cindy blurted out the moment Mark's phone picked up.

"We just figured out she's the girl in the picture the killer posted online," Mark said. "Where are you?"

"I'm two streets over from Sarah's. Jeremiah didn't want me nearby. He told me to drive over here and call you while he went into the house."

"Stay there, I'm on my way," Mark said.

The call disconnected and Cindy dropped the phone on the passenger seat. She drummed her fingers on the steering wheel, fidgeting. Not knowing what was happening in the house was killing her.

She checked for the tenth time that the car doors were locked. Jeremiah's paranoia had rubbed off on her. The irony of that would have made her laugh if she wasn't so scared for the girls.

She drummed the steering wheel harder as her anxiety mounted. Then she remembered one of the Christmas presents she'd gotten and she dove into her purse, pulling out a miniature deck of playing cards. She pulled them out of their plastic case. The slick surface of the cards felt good against her fingers. She tried to focus on that. When everything was spinning out of control if she could focus on one single tactile function then it would help calm her down. She began cutting the miniature cards one-handed. It took a little more concentration since she was working with a different size deck, but that was good. While she worked the cards in her left hand she began to pray.

~

Jeremiah was a living shadow, doing what he did best. The distress he'd been feeling for the last hour faded as he kept moving, coming closer to his objective. He had made it around to the back of Sarah's house unseen.

Though he'd seen no evidence of an alarm system he bypassed the back door and instead removed a screen and jimmied the window in the dining room. It slid open easily and after pausing a moment to listen he climbed noiselessly inside. Faint light came from the living room where he found a Christmas tree with several strands of lights blinking on and off. There, slumped under the tree, he found Sarah's mother.

He crouched swiftly, keeping his eyes glued on the rest of the room. He placed two fingers against her neck and felt her pulse. She was alive but unconscious.

He straightened and made his way to the staircase. At the bottom he hesitated, straining to see if he could hear anything upstairs. There was no sound at all. Every instinct in his body told him that danger waited at the top of the stairs. Still, he did not have the luxury of sitting back and waiting.

He started up slowly, gently testing each stair before putting his full weight on it. The least little squeak of a board could give him away and cost the girls their lives. He was halfway up when he felt a slight bit of give underneath his right foot. He could tell if he put pressure on the stair it would reveal his presence. He had no way of knowing, though, if the stair above it was sound.

He had to make a choice and the unknown stair was the lesser of two evils in that moment. He took a long step, bypassing the squeaky stair. His weight came down on the next stair up and he pushed off with his foot as he swung his other leg up.

The step groaned slightly.

Before Jeremiah could move a dark figure vaulted the railing on the second-floor landing and fell on him. Jeremiah fell backward, body swaying over empty air, then crashed down onto the stairs with the other man on top of him. They slid to the bottom where the other man locked his hands around Jeremiah's throat.

Jeremiah didn't bother to try and break the stranglehold. Instead he jabbed his thumbs upward sharply, aiming for the man's eyes. The other man snapped his head back and loosened his steely grip in the process.

Jeremiah punched toward his throat but the man rolled to the side and he only got in a glancing blow. Then the guy who had posed as Sarah's father was up and running. Jeremiah scrambled to his feet, ignoring the sharp pains in his back and shoulders which had taken the brunt of the fall.

The other man dove out the dining room window. Jeremiah made it there a dozen steps behind. Climbing out was much more difficult than climbing in had been thanks to his injuries. His feet touched down on the grass. Jeremiah raced toward the back of the house because that's the way he would have gone if he was fleeing.

He went over the fence into the back neighbor's yard. As soon as he landed a little dog ran toward him yapping. He had chosen the wrong direction since the dog hadn't been barking moments before. He climbed back over the fence. The murderer could have fled into the yards of either next door neighbor or into the street. It was too dark to look for tracks or trampled grass.

At this point he had less than a one in three chance of catching the guy. The better thing to do was go back inside and find Sarah and Brenda.

With an angry growl, he gave up and climbed back into the house through the open window. He hurried upstairs, his bruised body aching with every step. Once on the second floor it took only a moment to locate Sarah's room. Inside he found Brenda tied to a chair and gagged. Her wrists were raw from where she had been struggling against the ropes and she burst into tears when she saw Jeremiah.

He hurried to her and undid the gag before untying her. "Are you okay?" he asked.

"Yes, but he hit Sarah really hard," she burst out, pointing to the far side of the bed.

Jeremiah rounded it and found Sarah unconscious like her mom. There was a lump on her temple where the man had struck her. Anger coursed through Jeremiah as he stood up. The man who had hurt his girls was going to pay.

~

Cindy sat up straighter as she saw a figure emerge onto the street from between two houses. He was dressed in dark clothing and moving furtively. She reached for her cell with her right hand even as her left busily cut and recut her deck of cards. The figure ducked in front of a parked van, disappearing momentarily from her sight. She craned her neck, waiting to see where he went next.

There was a sudden pounding on her window and she jumped with a scream. Cards flew out of her hand to rain down all over the inside of the car.

"Sorry, didn't mean to scare you," Mark said.

She nodded and turned her eyes back to where she had last seen the man. There was no sign of him now. It was possible he was still in front of the truck, but deep down she knew he was gone.

"Have you heard from Jeremiah?" Mark asked impatiently.

"No," Cindy said.

She could hear sirens wailing in the distance. If their quarry didn't already know he was being hunted, he knew now. She closed her eyes and said another prayer for Jeremiah and the girls.

~

Two hours later Jeremiah and Cindy were once again headed back to Joseph and Geanie's house. Brenda, Sarah, and Sarah's mom had all been taken to the hospital under heavy police guard. Mark had tried to force Jeremiah to go, but he had refused. He needed to be free to move about and hunt down the killer.

Apparently, the killer had been waiting for the two girls in Sarah's room. They had gone straight upstairs upon entering the house and neither of them had seen Sarah's mom unconscious under the Christmas tree. He had knocked Sarah out and tied up Brenda. He had proceeded to bully and question her, stopping just short of physical violence. He was looking for something that he was convinced she had.

She had no idea what it was he was looking for, but she had told him that the rabbi was going to rescue them. He must have gotten spooked when Jeremiah actually showed up at the door because he hadn't returned to question Brenda more, but instead seemed to have been waiting for Jeremiah to return.

He'd been waiting for Jeremiah which is how he moved so quickly when the stair creaked. Fortunately, Brenda had felt confident in her ability to help a sketch artist put together a picture of him. That was a good thing, because the last thing Jeremiah wanted to do was spend more time with the police at that point.

"They're going to be okay," Cindy said softly.

She was driving. He was too distracted and in far too much pain to be driving if he didn't have to.

"I know," he said.

He just wished he'd accompanied them inside when they dropped them home. It had been careless. The killer had been waiting for them, though, which meant he hadn't followed them from Brenda's house. He'd found them by some other means.

When they finally made it back to the house, Jeremiah and Cindy trudged inside closely followed by Mark. As much as he wanted to get some food and some painkillers in his system immediately, Jeremiah still took a detour to the dining room to see how the Zone referees were doing.

As bad as Jeremiah felt, Mark looked worse. The detective looked dead on his feet, like he could collapse at any moment. He was under a tremendous amount of stress, and it was taking a toll.

"How are things going?" Mark asked wearily.

"I think I found something," Becca said.

Mark hurried over. He took one look at the computer screen and swore.

"What is it?" Jeremiah asked as he moved toward him.

"Recognize anyone?" Mark asked, waving at the screen.

There was a picture of Brenda talking to a man with a baseball cap pulled low over his eyes. While his face was partially obscured, the way he held himself was all too familiar.

Jeremiah took a step back, clenching his fists.

The man in the picture was Martin.

16

The next morning Jeremiah was sitting in the breakfast café in the World hotel. It was the hotel owned by the Zone. It was also the hotel that Cindy had stayed at when she was a juror. He was slowly sipping coffee and waiting. He'd been there about half an hour when he saw Martin walking through the lobby.

Jeremiah stared intently at him and Martin slowly turned his head, as though he could sense that he was being watched. He finally saw Jeremiah. He hesitated for a moment and then changed course. Moments later he was sitting down at Jeremiah's table.

"You're not hard to find," Jeremiah said, tightly controlling his voice and his facial expressions.

"I wasn't trying to be," Martin said. "Like I told you, I'm here on vacation with the family."

"I know you've been here longer than you made out when you came to visit me."

"Well, I wasn't looking to ruin either of our holidays. Besides, I was fairly certain our paths weren't going to cross. Then I saw that Kyle was filming at the park and I could no longer be certain of that."

The agent was being cagey. Jeremiah would have expected nothing less.

"Your little visit you paid me had nothing to do with Kyle filming in the park," Jeremiah said.

It was taking all he had not to start tearing the other man limb from limb since he was certain that the deaths of the cotton candy vendors had something to do with the spy.

"This should be entertaining. If it had nothing to do with Kyle, why else would I have bothered to warn you I was in town?"

"That's what I'm here to find out. We'll start by you telling me why there is surveillance footage of you and a cotton candy vendor named Brenda."

Until that moment the corners of Martin's mouth had been curled slightly upward in an almost smile. As Martin's eyes hardened, the faint smile disappeared.

"You do have to admit that for a rabbi you have quite a thing for church girls," Martin said, baiting him.

Jeremiah clenched his fists, struggling not to hit the agent. The fact that Martin knew that Brenda went to church showed that he knew something about her which precluded their meeting being a random encounter.

"I would choose your next words more carefully," Jeremiah said softly.

Martin leaned back in his chair and folded his arms across his chest.

"Interview is over when *I* say so, not you," Jeremiah warned.

"What do you want from me?" Martin asked. "I'm just a guy here on vacation."

"You see, that's fine, but I don't buy it," Jeremiah said. "What is the C.I.A.'s interest here?"

Martin sighed and leaned forward again. He lowered his voice.

"Look, I really am on vacation."

"But?" Jeremiah asked.

"But it turned out that we had an unexpected need for a field guy here."

"Your company isn't supposed to operate on American soil."

"Yeah, we all know that. Doesn't always work itself out that neat and pretty."

Jeremiah rolled his eyes. He had firsthand experience with that.

"So, what are you doing here, really?" Jeremiah asked.

"An asset was bringing us some crucial information. He was getting more and more paranoid, sure that he was being followed. He actually used a coyote to get across the border near San Diego. He contacted us and said he'd make the exchange only somewhere incredibly public. The Zone was his idea. I was already coming here on vacation. It was just an unhappy coincidence."

"Unhappy?"

"Yeah. When I'm with family I want to be *with* them, you know. Playing not working," Martin said.

Jeremiah nodded. Truthfully, he knew that men like Martin were almost never not working. Even if they were on vacation they were getting updates, being asked questions. The only time you truly got off was if you were injured badly enough to end up in the hospital.

"So, you made the exchange?"

Martin shook his head. "He hasn't showed and I'm getting concerned. It was my understanding that he was in the area before I arrived. I don't know, maybe he wasn't paranoid. Maybe someone was following him."

"What are you going to do?"

"We had a tracker on his phone, but he must have ditched it at some point."

"That's a best-case scenario," Jeremiah said.

"Yes, yes, it is," Martin admitted. "I'm trying to figure out where he might be or where he might have stashed the intel."

"That doesn't explain the cotton candy."

"Yeah, and I'm wondering how you knew about that," Martin said, narrowing his eyes.

"I've got friends in strange places."

Martin rolled his eyes.

"Don't we all."

"So?"

"Okay. We were able to retrieve some information from his phone before we lost the signal entirely. He had one picture on there. It was a blurry picture of a girl in a cotton candy vendor uniform."

Jeremiah felt himself go cold inside.

"Do you have a copy of this picture?" Jeremiah asked.

Martin pulled out his phone and showed Jeremiah the same picture of Brenda he'd seen the night before.

"Who else have you showed this picture to?" Jeremiah asked, his voice coming out in a low, rumbling growl.

"No one, why?"

"And does the name Kurt mean anything to you?"

"Not in the slightest. What's going on?" Martin asked.

Jeremiah studied the other man carefully. Martin was a trained spy. He was good at hiding the truth when it suited him. He was trying to assess whether Martin was lying to him now.

The night before, after Jeremiah had recognized Martin in the surveillance footage, Mark had filled him and Cindy in on everything that had happened with Kurt. Reports from the hospital that morning indicated that although he was in bad shape, the kid was going to pull through. It had been bad luck on his part that he had responded to the picture posted online and that the killer had been able to track him down. It really was a miracle he was still alive. Unfortunately, he hadn't yet regained consciousness so they didn't have any idea what the killer might have said or what Kurt had told him.

Jeremiah didn't think that Martin was lying about not knowing who Kurt was. It remained to be seen what exactly the other man did know about everything that was happening.

"You're not the only one with this picture," Jeremiah said. "The guy who's been killing the cotton candy girls has it, too."

Martin looked surprised.

"You think our asset has gone rogue and is killing girls?" Martin asked.

"You would know better than I," Jeremiah said.

"The guy's paranoid and a helluva thief, but he's not a killer. At least, that's my understanding."

"Then we should assume that the killer at least has hold of his phone."

"And probably him," Martin muttered.

"What's he smuggling for you?"

"Information."

"What kind?" Jeremiah pushed.

"Sorry, that's classified," Martin said quickly.

"You're going to need to be a little more forthcoming if you want my help."

"What makes you think I want your help?"

"Because you need it. Your asset is in the wind with some very sensitive information and someone is hunting him and might already have him. This is my town. I know it better than you," Jeremiah said. He leaned forward and lowered his voice. "And I am going to find whoever has been killing the cotton candy vendors. You've seen what happens when I go hunting. You know how it will end for everyone in the room, including your guy."

Martin's face had gone still, emotionless. It was like staring at a mask.

"You know, it's a good thing we're friends," Martin said, his voice cold.

"Are we?"

"I thought so until five minutes ago when you all but accused me of killing those girls," Martin said.

"I know you're capable of it."

"As are you. Not the point."

Over Martin's shoulder Jeremiah saw a five-year-old girl with wavy brown hair start to run across the lobby toward them. She entered the café and ran up behind Martin.

"Daddy! Mommy sent me to get you," she said as she came to a halt next to Martin and wrapped her arms around him.

Martin hoisted her up onto his lap with his left arm, but he kept his eyes locked on Jeremiah, his face expressionless.

"She said you'd be talking to a rabbi," the little girl said. "She also said to remind you we're having breakfast in the park. Hello, Mr. Rabbi, my name is Crystal."

"Nice to meet you, Crystal. I wasn't aware anyone knew I was here talking with your father."

"Mommy saw you an hour ago and told Daddy to come say hello."

"What can I say? She never forgets a face," Martin said.

"And yet I haven't had the pleasure of seeing hers," Jeremiah said.

"I intend to keep it that way for now."

Jeremiah could appreciate the awkward position Martin was in. Whatever he had told his wife about Jeremiah it had been such that she didn't mind sending their daughter into the restaurant.

"Are you finished saying hello?" Crystal asked.

"Yes, honey, we're finished," Martin said, still staring at Jeremiah.

"It was very nice to meet you, Crystal," Jeremiah said.

Crystal was regarding him with open curiosity. "You're one of Daddy's work friends, aren't you?" she asked.

Martin's face finally changed. He rolled his eyes and looked flustered and exasperated.

"Can't fool this one about anything," Martin muttered.

Crystal beamed. "I'm going to be a ann-a-list when I grow up. Either that or an operator," she said proudly. She leaned forward and whispered. "I know five different secret codes and how to shoot. I can hit the center of the paper man every time."

Martin turned red.

Jeremiah didn't know how to respond. He was pretty sure she was trying to say "analyst" and "operative". He knew Martin was an operative, so he was guessing that made the mother an analyst.

"It's an air gun," Martin muttered.

"Daddy says I can't have a Glock until my hands are big enough to hold it," Crystal said, holding up her hands. "I'm thinking for my eighth birthday."

"I'm thinking for your twelfth birthday."

Crystal laughed. "Daddy, you're so funny."

"And on that note, we have to go," Martin said.

He put Crystal down and stood up.

"Tell Mommy I'm coming," he said.

"Okay," Crystal said before scampering off.

Martin sighed.

"Kindergarten hasn't been easy. I got called in for three parent-teacher meetings last month," he said. "We're thinking maybe homeschooling is a better idea, at least until she doesn't feel the need to talk about target practice or the fact that she practices escaping from handcuffs, bungee cords, anything she can get her hands on. I swear, it's all her idea. Sometimes I wonder what she thinks I do for a living."

Jeremiah couldn't help himself. He started to laugh softly.

"Oh yeah? Just wait. Soon it will be your turn. Then you'll be the one stuck in the conferences with teachers and vice principals all wanting to know how come your kid took their throwing knives to show and tell."

"Maybe you shouldn't encourage her?"

"Encourage her? Who can stop her? At this point all I can do is teach her safety first and that we never, ever let anyone else touch our weapons."

Jeremiah started laughing harder.

"Of course, even that backfired," Martin said. "Her teacher tried to borrow one of Crystal's pencils and Crystal refused to let her have it. She told Miss Lewis that no one else was allowed to touch her weapons. When Miss Lewis informed Crystal that a pencil is not a weapon she argued with her. Crystal told her that the pencil is mightier than the sword and then proceeded to prove it by explaining how she could use the pencil to kill someone in three different ways."

"Four, actually," Jeremiah said.

"I know! And like an idiot, I said that when I heard the story," Martin said. "I'm pretty sure the principal thinks I'm some kind of serial killer now."

Jeremiah kept laughing. He could clearly picture the whole thing and he felt sorry for Martin.

"Hashtag spy parent problems, right? I keep telling myself it could be worse," Martin said.

"How?" Jeremiah asked.

"My wife's third cousin is an exorcist. When she has kids, I'm going to be right there to laugh and point when she gets called to school."

Martin stared into the distance, smiling slightly as he probably pictured that moment. Finally, he looked back at Jeremiah. "I'll share what I can when I can. Don't expect it will be much, but I'd appreciate you keeping me in the loop. And not shooting my guy if you find him."

"I wasn't planning on *shooting* him," Jeremiah said, with dark emphasis.

"Don't stab him either. Geesh, you're as bad as my daughter. I just wish I could put you in a timeout."

Before Jeremiah could respond, Martin turned and left. Jeremiah just sat for a minute, lost in thought. Martin's parental troubles were funny, but they also seemed a bit foreboding to him. Something that he'd thought about mostly in an abstract way was coming home to him full force, and he could feel himself beginning to panic slightly.

One day in the not so distant future, he and Cindy were going to have kids.

17

Jeremiah's phone buzzed and he retrieved it from his pocket. He'd received a text message from an unknown number. It was a picture of a man with dark hair, bright green eyes, and a hawkish nose. The picture was accompanied by three words: *Don't kill him*.

He was staring at a picture of Martin's asset, the man who had started this entire mess. Jeremiah rocketed to his feet and made a beeline for the exit. They might not need to find the killer if they could find the guy he was hunting. Then they could use the man for bait to draw the killer out before any more girls got hurt.

Once he made it back to his car he drove straight to the hospital. He arrived just a minute after Cindy who was sitting and talking with Brenda and Sarah. Both girls were in the same hospital room to make it easier for the police to concentrate their efforts in protecting them.

"Great timing. I just got here," Cindy said, giving him a smile.

Jeremiah nodded and did his best to keep his expression calm as he looked at the two girls.

Sarah was pale and had a bandage on her head from where the man had knocked her out. Relief swept over her face as she looked at him.

"Rabbi, I feel safer already," she said. "Thank you for saving us."

"We knew you would," Brenda added with a wan smile.

For having been questioned by a killer the night before she looked really good.

"How are you both feeling?" he asked. He was impatient to show Brenda the picture that Martin had sent him, but he forced himself to pause first. He didn't want to traumatize the girls any more than they already had been. At the moment what they most needed was comfort and reassurance. He would need to tread carefully.

"My head was throbbing when I woke up, but they gave me some pain killers and I'm okay," Sarah said.

"Any concussion?"

"The doctor said I had a little one, but that it's not anything to worry about," she said. She smiled faintly. "Nothing a Ranger can't handle."

He smiled reassuringly.

"Rangers are as tough as they come," he said, feeling a swell of pride as he did so. He turned to Brenda. "And how are you doing?" he asked.

"I'm trying to figure out how I should be doing," she admitted.

"There's no right or wrong way to feel," Cindy said softly.

Cindy reached out to grip Brenda's hand and Jeremiah turned his head so Brenda wouldn't see the tears that suddenly sprang to his eyes. Cindy had been through so much trauma, more than anyone should ever have to bear. Instead of breaking her, though, it had made her stronger. Strong enough to advise and comfort others and to do so without giving way to the darkness or the anxiety herself.

Once upon a time it would have been a different story. She had changed.

Almost as much as I have, he realized.

Once, not that long ago, it would have been unthinkable, laughable even, for him to contemplate the fact that he'd have a fiancée, friends, and a crazy hodgepodge of personalities that he called family.

"I mean, I know I should be upset and scared," Brenda said. "And part of me is, but the whole time I knew it was going to be okay. I knew you'd come and save us," she said, looking directly at Jeremiah.

He winced when he thought about how close he'd come to just calling it a night and not pressing. If Marie hadn't come through with the information she had, he might not have gone back. The pressure he felt in that moment was overwhelming. What if he wasn't there for Brenda and Sarah the next time?

He glanced at Cindy. What if he wasn't there for her? He wasn't G-d. He couldn't be everywhere at once.

It wasn't the first time he'd struggled with this, but it was the first time he really let himself understand that he was responsible for far more than just the woman he intended to marry. His friends, his congregation, the Rangers all relied on him in ways he couldn't have anticipated.

"I'm sorry I wasn't there sooner," he said hoarsely.

"You were there when you were needed," Brenda said. "I think things were going to get a lot worse, but he kept acting all fidgety, going to check and see if you were coming like I told him you were. He only really asked me three or four questions after he tied me to the chair."

Jeremiah winced, remembering how she'd looked when he found her.

"What did he ask?" Cindy said, leaning forward eagerly.

She was on the case, determined to find out the truth. He felt a surge of warmth as he watched her. She'd really missed her calling. Although if he suggested to her that she should be a private detective he was pretty sure she would laugh and Mark would have a fit.

And I'd spend every second worrying.

Not that he didn't do that already. Of course, some days were worse than others.

"He kept asking me about some guy named Nikola. I told him the truth. I don't know any Nikola," Brenda said.

"What else did he ask you?" Cindy said.

"He kept saying I had to know Nikola and that he gave me something. It didn't make any sense. Then he went on about how he knew I was the right one because of my shoes."

"Your shoelaces, actually," Jeremiah said.

"The ones Becca gave me?" Brenda asked, looking bewildered.

"That's right," Jeremiah said.

"I don't understand," Brenda said.

"What do her shoelaces have to do with anything?" Sarah asked.

"Someone was looking for a cotton candy vendor, but they didn't have a picture of her face. However, you could make out shoelaces and they were Brenda's," Cindy said.

Jeremiah pulled the picture of the man he was guessing was Nikola up on his phone. He handed it to Brenda.

"Did you see him, probably in the park?" Jeremiah asked.

Brenda took the phone with a frown and studied the picture. She nodded slowly. "Yes, he bought cotton candy from me a few days ago."

She handed the phone back to Jeremiah.

"Who is he?" she asked.

"This might be Nikola," Jeremiah said.

"Oh," Brenda said, her eyes widening.

Cindy was looking at Jeremiah in surprise, but he didn't want to discuss his conversation with Martin in front of the girls.

"Did he say anything to you?" Jeremiah asked.

"Not really," Brenda said, frowning.

"Please think," Cindy said. "Anything, no matter how insignificant, could be important at this point."

Jeremiah nodded agreement.

"He came up to me, said he'd like one cotton candy. Just like a hundred other people."

"And then?" Cindy urged.

"Nothing. I told him how much. He gave me some money and I gave him his change. I was excited because he had handed me some dollar bills and a dollar coin. I told him I collect dollar coins and he didn't say anything which was a bit rude. I handed him his cotton candy and that was it."

"Nothing else, you're sure?" Cindy asked.

"Oh, someone dropped a receipt. I think it was him, but I'm not sure. I saw it about two minutes after he left. It was for breakfast at Sunny Side Up which is all the way across town."

"What did you do with the receipt?" Jeremiah asked.

"I threw it away at the end of my shift. I figured no one would care."

"Was there a name on it, like for a credit card payment?" Jeremiah asked.

"No, it was a cash payment," Brenda said. "Why? Do you think the receipt was important?"

"It might be," Jeremiah said.

"I know the restaurant. It's not that far away from the synagogue. Mom and I eat lunch there sometimes on Sundays," Sarah piped up. "A week ago Brenda was there with us."

"That's right," Brenda said with a nod. "After lunch they dropped me off at work."

Cindy looked at Jeremiah. He could see the curiosity burning in her eyes.

"Maybe we should go check it out," Cindy said.

"Maybe so," Jeremiah agreed.

"You think you'll find him there?" Brenda asked.

"If we're lucky," Jeremiah said.

"Then go," Sarah urged.

Jeremiah hesitated.

"We're fine," Brenda assured him. "Just go find Nikola and maybe he'll help you catch the guy who did this to us."

Jeremiah stood. After a moment Cindy did, too.

"Looks like we have our marching orders," she said with a smile.

"Yes, please find out who did this," Sarah urged.

"You're sure you'll be okay?" Jeremiah asked, having really mixed feelings about leaving them again given what had happened the night before.

"They'll be fine," Mark said as he entered the room. "We've got half a dozen officers on this floor. That's how I knew you two were here." Mark looked at the girls. "Ladies, I'll be in to speak with you in a few minutes."

"Okay," Brenda said.

"Rabbi, Cindy, a word outside," Mark said, stepping back out of the doorway.

Jeremiah and Cindy followed him halfway down the hallway before he stopped.

"What's going on?" he asked.

"That's what we're trying to find out," Cindy said.

"So, something was bugging me this morning," Mark said. "Why go to the bother of tying up Brenda and questioning her? Especially given that he probably knew from talking to Kurt that she was the cotton candy girl he was looking for. I mean, he just killed the other two. Why not just kill her?"

Jeremiah felt his hands curling into fists at his side at the thought of the man who had attacked him killing Brenda.

"That's a good point," Cindy said. "I hadn't thought about it."

"Did you come up with an answer?" Jeremiah asked.

"Partially. I talked to forensics this morning. Turns out the girl who was killed in my backyard did run there from down the street. It looks like he followed her home from work. There were signs at her house of a struggle in the garage. I think he tried to question her and she struggled and got away. She ran. He caught her. Whether or not he meant to kill her right then and there or he just applied too much pressure we don't know. But there is evidence that they were probably in her garage for ten minutes before she got away."

"Why didn't she run into the house and call 911?" Cindy asked.

"That I don't know."

"Even if he did question her, what about the girl in The Zone?" Jeremiah asked.

"An excellent point, which is why I said I only partially had an answer," Mark said.

"Well, it's more than we had earlier," Cindy said. "According to Brenda, the guy last night kept asking her if she knew someone named Nikola. She said she didn't, but a minute ago she acknowledged selling cotton candy to someone who might be Nikola," Cindy said, turning to look at Jeremiah inquisitively.

Jeremiah showed Mark the picture.

"Okay, who is this guy and why does our killer care if she knows him?" Mark asked.

"Apparently, he's a C.I.A. asset that Martin was supposed to rendezvous with in The Zone," Jeremiah said.

Jeremiah couldn't tell whether Mark or Cindy looked more upset when he mentioned the agent. He couldn't blame either of them given their last encounter with him.

"I knew it! I knew it when I saw that picture of him last night," Mark said, scowling.

"You were able to track him down this morning?" Cindy asked.

"It wasn't hard," Jeremiah said.

"And he gave you the picture?" she asked.

He nodded.

"Does he know why the killer is going after the cotton candy girls?" Mark asked.

"No, but I think our earlier theory that one of them saw or heard something she shouldn't have is a sound one," Jeremiah said.

"We're on our way to check out a restaurant Nikola ate at before he bought cotton candy from Brenda," Cindy said.

"You need me to send anyone with you?" Mark asked.

Jeremiah shook his head.

"Probably just as well. I hate having to explain those type of things," Mark muttered.

"We'll let you know what we find," Cindy said.

"You better. I want to know as soon as you know," Mark said. "We've all landed in one awful mess and we need to be on our toes from here on out."

Jeremiah thought of asking how Traci was doing, but a clock was ticking in his mind. They didn't have a lot of time before the man they were hunting tried something else in an effort to get to Brenda or any of the other girls. So, instead he just nodded, grabbed Cindy's hand, and left Mark standing in the hallway muttering to himself.

~

"Are you okay?" Cindy asked Jeremiah as soon as they were in his car.

"I'm worried," he admitted.

"I know. Hopefully we'll find Nikola and get all this taken care of," she said.

She seriously doubted they'd be lucky enough to stumble across Nikola at the restaurant, but it was the only lead they had, and they needed to check it out. Both of them were tense. She wasn't in the mood for small talk and it seemed neither was he. They spent the twenty minutes it took to get to the restaurant mostly in silence. Finally, Jeremiah parked in the Sunny Side Up parking lot.

As it turned out the restaurant was right in front of a budget motel. Cindy wasn't one hundred percent sure if the two were connected or not.

"Can I see the picture of Nikola? I didn't get a good look when you showed it to Brenda," she said.

Jeremiah handed her his phone and she worked to fix the face in the picture in her mind so she'd know it if she saw him. She handed the phone back after a few seconds.

"Do you think he's staying at the motel?" she asked.

"It would make sense," Jeremiah said. "No other reason for him to be eating breakfast all the way out here if The Zone was his intended meeting place."

"Okay, let's do this," she said.

They walked inside the restaurant which wasn't very busy.

"Two?" the hostess asked.

"Actually, we're looking for a friend of ours, Nikola. We're supposed to meet him for breakfast," Cindy said, putting on her most innocent look and hoping it worked.

"What's he look like?" the hostess asked.

"Dark hair, green eyes." Cindy leaned in and lowered her voice. "He's got a large, pretty distinctive nose."

The hostess' eyes lit up in recognition.

"Oh, that guy! Yeah. He was in here several times last week, but I haven't seen him the last few days," she said.

Cindy tried to keep cool, not wanting to draw undue attention. She chewed her lip. "He's not picking up his cell. Do you know if his hotel has phones in the room?"

It sounded like a lame thing to say, particularly since she'd never seen or heard of a hotel that didn't.

The hostess chuckled. "I know the motel doesn't look fancy, but we've got the bare necessities. If you go into the lobby they can ring his room for you."

"Thanks," Cindy said, giving the woman a big smile.

Jeremiah had his phone out and looked to be texting someone. He followed Cindy out of the restaurant and into the motel lobby. The place was neat looking, even if all the furnishings were dated.

As she walked up to the desk she wondered what she'd say to convince the attendant to ring the room of someone whose last name she didn't have. She smiled, hoping to come off as confident.

"Can I help you?" the guy behind the desk asked.

"Yes. I was talking to a very nice guy who came by one of our events at church today. He left and I realized he'd left his cell phone behind. His name is Nikola. He's new in town, and he's staying here, and I just want to get it back to him," Cindy said.

The guy hesitated, looking uncertain. The phone on his desk suddenly rang.

"Excuse me one moment."

He picked it up and Cindy turned to Jeremiah. He looked at her and smiled.

"What?" she asked softly. She could tell he was up to something. She just didn't know what.

"Um, okay," the clerk said before hanging up. He looked at them in a mixture of awe and dread. "I'm sorry. I didn't know who you were."

"That's okay," Jeremiah said. "The room number?"

"Right away," he said, punching up something on the computer. "It's 412. Let me get you a key."

"Thank you," Jeremiah said.

Moments later they had left the lobby and were heading toward room 412.

"Okay, what happened back there?" Cindy asked.

"I thought you did a fantastic job with your cover story," he said.

"Thanks, but clearly it was whatever happened on that phone call that convinced the guy to help. So, spill. How did you manage that?"

"Friends in strange places," Jeremiah said with a chuckle.

She was about to ask him what on earth he meant by that when he nodded to a door.

"Here we are," he said. "Better stand to the side in case this guy's jumpy."

Cindy nodded and stood a few feet back.

Jeremiah knocked loudly on the door then paused, listening. He shook his head and she gathered that he didn't hear anything.

Using the key, Jeremiah opened the door. He stepped inside then froze. She walked forward, but Jeremiah turned around, blocking her view of the interior of the room.

"Don't come any closer," he said.

"What is it?"

"There's a dead body," he said. "You don't want to look."

"I've seen dead bodies before," she said, taking a deep breath.

"Not like this. He was tortured."

18

It was the first time since the day in the church sanctuary that Cindy found a dead body and Mark didn't show up. Instead it was Martin, the C.I.A. agent, who came after Jeremiah called him.

"I told you not to kill him," Martin said when he arrived.

"I didn't," Jeremiah said. "But whoever did wanted something pretty badly."

Cindy was leaning against the wall of the motel a couple doors down from the room with the body. She watched as Martin walked in then walked right back out. She was trying not to breathe too deeply as there was a strong stench coming from the room.

Martin looked upset when he came out.

"He's been dead at least three or four days," he said.

"Agreed," Jeremiah responded.

"His phone's gone. You're right. Whoever killed him grabbed the only picture on it of the girl."

"Brenda. Her name is Brenda and last night the killer tied her up and began questioning her. He was convinced she'd had contact with your guy in there. Turns out she did. She sold him some cotton candy a few days ago," Jeremiah said.

"And?" Martin asked.

"And that's it," Jeremiah said.

"I don't buy it," Martin said, shaking his head. "Nikola wouldn't have bothered taking her picture if she wasn't significant in some way."

"She's just a sweet girl who goes to my church," Cindy said, speaking up. "She was in the wrong place at the wrong time."

"For selling cotton candy?" Martin asked, voice dripping sarcasm. "Look, even if she is exactly who you say she is, there's more to the story."

"She's a scared young girl," Jeremiah said, his voice a growl.

"Fine, but she knows something. She might not realize it, but she does. Otherwise Nikola wouldn't have taken a picture of her and his killer wouldn't be after her," Martin insisted. "I want to talk to her."

"No," Cindy and Jeremiah said at the exact same time.

"No?" Martin asked incredulously.

"You heard us," Cindy said. "She's already been through enough. She doesn't need to get swept up in whatever this is," she said, waving her hand to indicate the room and Martin.

"How do I break this to you, Cindy? She's already swept up in whatever this is," he said, making an exaggerated circle to indicate all of them. "And if you want to get her safely out of this, then you'll let me talk to her."

"So you can imprison her or get her killed?" Cindy asked hotly.

Martin looked like he was about to lose his temper. He turned to Jeremiah. "Talk to her," he said. "You know this is in the girl's best interest and you owe me."

Cindy seethed. She knew that her last encounter with Martin, where he'd put her and all their friends plus her family in protective custody, had been at Jeremiah's request. Still, she couldn't bear Jeremiah ill will for that, so she was going to blame Martin for it. She knew it wasn't fair or necessarily even rational, but it was how she was feeling.

"By my count, you owe us," Cindy snapped.

Martin strode forward until he was inches from her. He stared into her eyes. "I was on your side in Tehran."

Before she could respond he walked past her. She could hear him call someone but within moments he was out of range, and she couldn't hear what he was saying.

"As long as the killer thinks Brenda has something or knows something, she's going to be in danger," Jeremiah said softly.

"I know," Cindy said, feeling miserable. She hated that the girl was in danger. It would have been so much easier if it had been her. She was used to being in danger. She wasn't sure when exactly that had come to feel normal to her, but on some level it had.

"It's too late for me to dress up like a cotton candy girl and play decoy, isn't it?" she asked Jeremiah.

He smiled and moved closer. "It is, but you would have made an awfully cute decoy."

"Thanks," she said, wondering what was wrong with her that his observation made her feel better.

"We have no idea what exactly the killer might be looking for. Martin might."

"Then make him tell us so we can find it," she said.

He chuckled. "Last time I checked, neither of us worked for the C.I.A.," he said.

"Your point being?"

"We don't have clearance to know and he doesn't have the ability to tell us."

"Doesn't mean I have to like it," she said.

"No, it doesn't," he said, kissing the tip of her nose.

She couldn't stop herself from smiling. He smiled back.

"You think we should let him talk to Brenda," she said.

"I do."

"Then why did you say 'no' when I did?"

"Knee-jerk response. I want to protect her, but he's right. She's already involved in this. The best thing we can do for her is to figure this out quickly, so she can go back to living her life without a police protection detail hovering over her shoulder."

"You make a lot of sense sometimes," Cindy admitted.

"Only sometimes?"

"Don't push it."

"You feeling any better?" he asked.

"Except for one thing," she admitted.

"What's that?"

"I would really like to move away from the smell."

~

Half an hour later Jeremiah was driving back to the hospital. Cindy was in the passenger seat and Martin was following in his own car. Martin's colleagues had arrived to lock down the scene at the motel. When and if they would call in the local police was not Jeremiah's concern. Although he was fairly certain Mark would prefer to be left out of the mess, particularly given Martin's involvement.

Jeremiah was surprised to find that Mark was still at the hospital. He was waiting in the room with Sarah and

181

Brenda. He got to his feet the moment Cindy and Jeremiah walked through the door.

"How did it-"

Mark froze mid-sentence as Martin walked in behind them. His face turned white and for a moment Jeremiah thought the detective was going to explode.

"Good to see you again, Detective," Martin said with a cool nonchalance that Jeremiah could tell was eating Mark alive.

"I wish I could say the same," Mark said.

Mark glared daggers first at Martin then at Jeremiah.

"It's for the best," Jeremiah said, trying to reassure the other man.

"For who exactly?" Mark asked.

"Everyone," Martin said. "Personal feelings aside. By the way, Jeremiah, remind me to send you a nice gift basket as a thank you for making sure that all of your friends and I are on such great terms," he added sarcastically.

"Everyone play nice," Jeremiah said.

"Rabbi, who is this?" Sarah asked, sitting up.

"A friend who is here to help," Jeremiah said.

"I'm going to go get some coffee," Mark said.

"Don't let us stop you," Martin said.

Mark walked out looking angry.

"Problem?" Jeremiah asked under his breath.

"Had to threaten to kill him to get him to behave. You know how it is," Martin said so softly only Jeremiah could hear.

"Been there," Jeremiah muttered.

"Brenda, you can call me Martin. Rabbi Silverman and I are old friends," Martin said as he pulled a chair up next to Brenda's bed. "How are you feeling?"

"I'm okay," she said. "I want to get out of here."

"Everyone's always in a rush to leave hospitals," Martin said with a grin. "The trick I've found is to treat it like a mini-vacation. As long as you're in here no one can ask you to do anything. No work, no chores, there's absolutely no expectations on you."

Brenda smiled. "You're weird."

"It's been said. Now, I know that you don't want to really dwell on this too much, so I'm going to try and make this as fast as I can."

"Okay."

"Rabbi Silverman tells me that you sold some cotton candy to the man he showed you a picture of. His name is Nikola."

Jeremiah noted that Martin didn't use the past tense when saying that. He clearly didn't plan on telling Brenda that Nikola was dead.

"Yes, I did," Brenda said.

"Good. Now, I want you to think. Did he look worried or upset in any way?"

"He looked kind of impatient I guess."

"How so?" Martin asked.

"He kept looking over his shoulder, like he was waiting for someone or like he had somewhere he had to be."

"Good, that's excellent. Did he look over both shoulders or just one?"

"Both, actually. I think he was expecting someone."

"Okay, you're doing great. Where you were in the park, what was behind him?"

"We were in the front of the Splash Zone."

"That's toward the back of the park, right?"

"Yes. I was near the front of the line for the Kowabunga ride. So, I was facing toward the walkway that leads to The Extreme Zone. Behind him there wasn't much of anything until you get to the bridge to the next zone."

"So, a pretty wide-open space," Martin said.

"Yes."

"Did he look like he spotted whoever he was looking for?"

"No."

"So, after he bought the cotton candy from you, which direction did he go?"

"Toward the Exploration Zone."

"Did he approach you from that direction?"

"No, he came from the Thrill Zone and then headed toward the Exploration Zone."

"How fast was he walking when he came up to you?" Martin asked.

"Pretty fast," she said. "For a moment I thought he was going to ask me where to find a restroom."

"Oh, because he looked uncomfortable, like there was some kind of urgency."

"Yeah, you know, that little dance people do when they really have to go," she said with a smile.

"I've danced that one many times myself," Martin said with a smile. "But he didn't ask you about the bathroom?"

"No. He just said he'd take one cotton candy."

"Okay. Now, when he walked away, did he have that same urgent look?"

Brenda paused.

"No, he didn't," she finally said. "He walked quickly, but not like he had to go, you know?"

"Yes."

Jeremiah exchanged a look with Cindy. She was clearly impressed by the amount of information Martin was extracting seemingly effortlessly. It certainly was telling that Nikola had been more anxious approaching Brenda's cart than leaving it.

"Okay, Brenda, did you actually see him eat any of the cotton candy?" Martin asked.

"No, actually. I guess that's a little weird. Usually people start eating as soon as they get it," she said.

Martin nodded. "Did he say anything else to you besides the fact that he wanted to purchase one cotton candy?"

"Not a word. Not even thank you. Most people say that when you hand them something, you know?"

"That was rude of him. He can be that way sometimes," Martin said.

"I remember you," Brenda blurted out suddenly.

"Pardon?" Martin asked.

"I think you bought cotton candy from me the other day."

"I did," Martin said, giving her a faint smile. "Apparently I was not as memorable as my friend Nikola."

"It was his nose. It looked like a hawk or something, the way it was hooked. Plus, he paid with a silver dollar, so I was paying more attention," Brenda said.

"He did, huh?"

"Yes, four dollar bills and one silver dollar."

"Scrounging for change, was he?" Martin asked.

Jeremiah noticed a subtle change in the spy's posture. He was leaning in slightly more, as though ready to pounce on Brenda's next word.

"No. He actually had more dollar bills, but he deliberately only paid with four and then the coin. I guess he got sick of hauling it around. They are heavy."

"And you noticed this coin because…" Martin said, trailing off.

"Oh, that's easy. I collect them," Brenda said with a smile. "You don't see them that often, but I always try to get one when I see it."

"And how do you get it?" Martin asked.

"I keep a dollar bill in my pocket, just in case. If someone pays with a dollar coin, I just swap my bill for the coin in the register."

Martin's entire body had gone incredibly still.

"And how often does that happen?"

"It's fairly rare, but that was a good day. Not that long before one of my friends in the park had brought me one. Everyone knows I collect them, so they keep an eye out for me."

Martin glanced up at Jeremiah and caught his gaze. He nodded slightly and so did Jeremiah. It was a decades old German trick for smuggling microfilm. Place what you were carrying inside a seemingly ordinary object. It was something that a man who was worried he was being followed might do.

And in this case, Nikola had.

Martin turned back to Brenda.

"Brenda, where is that coin now?" he asked.

"Why?" she asked, clearly surprised. "Is the coin important?"

"Yes."

"It's in my purse which is back at Sarah's house."

"Thank you," Martin said, standing abruptly.

Martin headed for the door and nearly collided with Mark who entered carrying a cup of coffee.

"Whoa, where are you heading in such a hurry?" Mark asked.

"To retrieve a coin before anyone else can," Martin said.

"A coin, is it valuable or something?"

"It's worth killing for."

19

"We'll take my car," Jeremiah said as he caught up to Martin in the parking lot.

"We?" Martin asked.

"Yeah. Like it or not I'm in the middle of this. Plus, you don't know where Sarah lives."

"Bet me," Martin said.

"I don't have to use the GPS to get there," Jeremiah amended.

"Fine," Martin said.

A minute later they were driving down the road. Jeremiah glanced over at the other man.

"Even if you find what you're looking for, that only solves half our problem."

"I'm aware," Martin said. His watch flashed. He glanced at it and sighed heavily.

"Work?" Jeremiah asked.

"Wife. Normally far preferable."

"But?"

"She wants to know how much longer I'm stuck at work. And don't laugh. Here, but for the grace of God, go you."

"I wouldn't dream of it," Jeremiah said. "Truth is, when I was in that line of work, I never even dreamed a personal life would be possible."

"Not probable, but possible," Martin said distractedly. "What would it take to get you to actually step on it?"

Jeremiah chuckled. "Always ready for an invitation," he said.

He depressed the accelerator and the car leaped forward. He kept his eyes moving, checking for other cars, pedestrians, and police. The truth was that he felt more comfortable driving faster. It engaged all his senses and let him focus.

"Are we there yet?" Martin asked after a minute.

"Yes, we're just looking for parking."

"Very funny."

Five minutes later they arrived at Sarah's house. The front door was blocked off with crime scene tape. Sarah's mom was still at the hospital, just in a different room than the girls. He needed to check in on her when he got back. It was going to be a bit awkward, though. She knew that he had been the one to scare off the intruder. What he didn't know was just how much Sarah had told her mother about the events at Green Pastures. He guessed he was about to find out. It was getting harder and harder to keep a low profile in the town.

They got out of the car and walked up to the door. They ducked under the tape and Martin pulled a lockpick set out of his pocket. Seconds later he was opening the door. They walked inside, closing the door behind them.

"Brenda's purse?" Martin asked.

"Probably upstairs in Sarah's room," Jeremiah said.

He moved to the staircase and led the way up. Even though he tried to step as gently as possible, every stair was a jarring reminder of how he'd landed on his back on it the night before.

"Old football injury?" Martin asked, clearly noticing that Jeremiah was struggling.

"Sure," Jeremiah said sarcastically. "Although here in the states I believe you call it soccer."

Martin actually chuckled at that.

"I'm trying to picture you as a goalie," he admitted.

"That's your area. I was more of a striker," Jeremiah said.

At the top of the stairs they turned and moments later were in Sarah's room. He recognized Brenda's backpack in the corner and picked it up. He put it on the bed and unzipped it. Inside he found clothes, a toiletry bag, and finally a purse. He hesitated before opening it.

"You are kidding me, right?" Martin asked. "You were a spy for how many years and you have trouble going through a girl's purse?"

"I know the girl," Jeremiah snapped. "And while malakh ha-mavet might not have a problem going through someone's purse, Rabbi Silverman most certainly does."

"Fair enough," Martin said. "Give it here."

Jeremiah reluctantly handed him the purse.

"I don't envy you having to live a fake identity," Martin said as he unzipped the purse.

"It's not fake," Jeremiah said reflexively. At least, that's what he told himself every day.

"Poor choice of words," Martin said as he pulled a coin pouch out of the purse. Inside were three silver dollars. He hefted each in his hand and then held one aloft. "Got it," he said.

The relief in his voice was clear.

"Care to tell me what all this fuss has been about?" Jeremiah asked.

"Not even if I could," Martin said fervently.

Whatever it was, it clearly made him nervous. Jeremiah had seen a lot of different sides of Martin, but not this one before. He put the coin pouch back in the purse, zipped it up, and handed it back to Jeremiah who returned it to the backpack.

They left the room and headed downstairs. They made it to the first floor and were walking to the front door when the hair on the back of Jeremiah's neck stood on end. Martin suddenly swiveled his head, as though listening for something.

Jeremiah started to slow but Martin shook his head slightly.

"Too bad there was nothing here," Martin said. "The girl's got to know where the microfilm is," he said, a little more loudly than normal.

He wants to be overheard, Jeremiah realized.

"Yeah, but what can we do? She's in the hospital," Jeremiah said.

"I talked to a doctor who told me she's going to be released this afternoon. She should be back here tonight. Maybe we wait until three in the morning and then pay her a little visit and get the truth out of her. I'm telling you, she knows more than she's letting on."

They exited the house, locking the front door as they did so. They ducked back under the police tape and hurried to the car.

"I don't know where he was, but I could feel him watching us downstairs," Martin said once they had driven down the street.

"Me, too," Jeremiah admitted. "So, you figure he'll be here after the girls get home but well before three to try and get the answer himself?"

"That's right."

~

Cindy's patience was stretched to the breaking point. Candace had shown up shortly after Jeremiah and Martin left, providing a much-needed distraction. Mark had been in and out of the room, alternately talking to the girls and fielding questions from other officers. She could practically feel the tension coming off him. He was as impatient for news as she was.

She was about to call Jeremiah when he walked into the hospital room. She rocketed to her feet.

"Did you find it?" she asked.

Jeremiah nodded.

"Where's Martin?"

"Taking care of a few things. And we need to as well."

"Like what?" Candace asked, standing up from her chair.

"We've been setting a trap for the... man we're trying to catch," Jeremiah said, pausing awkwardly in mid-sentence.

He didn't want to say the word "killer" in front of the girls, Cindy realized.

"What can we do to help?" Cindy asked.

"Well, we need to make it look like Sarah and Brenda are being discharged, just in case he's watching."

"Aren't we being discharged?" Brenda piped up.

"Not yet," Jeremiah said. "You need to stay here one more night."

Cindy could tell that it was a safety requirement and not a medical one that would be delaying the girls' release.

"So, we make it look like they've been discharged, then what?" she asked.

"Then we catch the man when he shows up at Sarah's house tonight hoping to get more information out of Brenda."

"Then don't I kind of need to be there?" Brenda asked, looking pale and resolute.

"Me, too?" Sarah asked.

Jeremiah shook his head. "It's too risky to have you girls waiting. We'll try to make it seem like you're at the house even though you won't be."

Cindy knew that was a bad idea. The man they were dealing with had already slipped through Jeremiah's fingers once. They couldn't risk him doing that again.

"You're going to need a decoy," Cindy said quietly.

From the look on his face she could tell that he thought so as well.

"So, I volunteer," she said, forcing a smile onto her face.

"You can't do that," he said.

"Yes, I can. Brenda and I are about the same height and build. If I get a wig and wear her clothes, he won't know it's me until it's too late."

"You need me, too," Sarah said. "Otherwise he'd get suspicious if he thought Brenda was going back to my house alone instead of just going to her house or staying here another night with me."

"She has a point," Cindy admitted grudgingly.

"There's no way I'm letting you risk it," Jeremiah said to Sarah.

"But Rabbi's Rangers-"

"Need to sit this one out," he said, interrupting her.

"I'll do it," Candace said quietly.

Cindy turned to look at her. "You can't. It's going to be too dangerous."

"It can't be overly dangerous or your fiancé wouldn't let you do it," Candace pointed out. "Besides, I'm roughly Sarah's size."

"Alright, it's settled," Cindy said.

She didn't like the idea of the young woman putting herself in danger, but at this point it was better that she do it than they put Sarah or Brenda back into the fray.

"It could get rough," Jeremiah warned.

Candace took a deep breath. "They built the Candy Craze maze off my legend. I can do it."

"Okay," Jeremiah said. "I'll get the wigs."

At that moment Mark walked into the room. He scowled.

"What on earth did I miss?" Mark asked.

~

Mark didn't like using his friends as bait. Still, for the plan to work they didn't really have a choice. He also didn't like running a joint op with Martin. Then again, it was only a joint operation in the loosest sense of the word. Mark, Liam, and Lou were the only three Pine Springs officers who would be involved. As it was, Lou's involvement was going to be minimal. It would be his job to drive the decoys from the hospital to the house, then park outside and pretend to fall asleep.

Of course, it was possible that Lou might *actually* fall asleep. One way or another, though, the killer had to view him as a non-threat.

The time finally came and Mark and Liam watched from their car as Lou helped first Cindy then Candace into his car at the hospital entrance. The disguises had turned out to be really good. With wigs and the borrowed clothes the two women bore passing resemblances to Brenda and Sarah.

Mark drove off as soon as both women were in the car. He didn't know if the killer was somewhere close by watching and would notice if anyone else was following the car. It was just as likely that he was avoiding the hospital and keeping his eyes completely fixed on the house.

"I'm worried about Geanie and Joseph," Liam said as soon as they turned out of the hospital parking lot.

"So am I," Mark said.

Liam paused for several seconds before speaking again. "I don't think you are. Not nearly enough, at any rate."

"Excuse me?" Mark asked, surprised.

"I think they're in real trouble. And since we're the ones who got them into it, we need to be doing everything in our power to get them out of it."

"Like what?" Mark asked, anger rising. "Tell me what is in our power to do that we haven't done yet."

"I don't know, but there has to be something," Liam said, frustration filling his voice.

"Look, I hear you, I really do. But one crisis at a time. This, right here, is what's on fire. We put it out and we deal with the next fire."

"You can't blame me for wanting to prevent the fires instead of being forced to scramble to put them out."

"No, but there's only so many hours in the day and only so many things we can control," Mark said. "And right now getting Cindy and Candace through tonight safe and sound is our priority. We'll deal with the next thing tomorrow. We might not like it, but that's how it is."

Liam muttered something under his breath but didn't say anything for the rest of the drive. He finally pulled over on the block behind Sarah's and turned off the engine.

"That's the house?" Liam asked, pointing through the side yard of the house facing them to the one behind it.

"Yes, that's Sarah's house," Mark said. "Now all we have to do is wait."

He hated that they were so far from the action, but if the killer escaped and fled they needed to be in a position to cut him off and this was the best bet. Plus, they didn't want to draw attention to themselves by having everyone park on Sarah's street.

"Cindy and Candace should be arriving in two minutes," Mark said. "Then it's showtime."

~

"I think I need to rethink my life choices," Cindy said to herself as the car carrying her and Candace slowed down and stopped in front of Sarah's house.

"Days like this, you're preaching to the choir," Candace said.

"And other days?" Cindy asked.

"Other days I think I have the most amazing life ever and I want to pinch myself," Candace said.

"Okay, ladies. I will escort you to the house. Hang onto each other, hang tough and we'll all get through this," Lou said. "Remember, keep your heads down and huddle together like you're scared."

"That last part will be easy," Candace said.

Cindy reached out and squeezed her hand. "We'll be fine," she said, hoping she sounded more confident than she felt.

"Time to go," Lou said.

It was dusk outside, so visibility was going to be low. Lou came around and opened the back door for them and they got out and then hurried to the front door. Once inside they closed and locked the door.

"I wish Lou was in here with us," Candace said.

"Me, too," Cindy admitted.

"Let's go upstairs and get settled in," Candace said.

Together they made it upstairs and into Sarah's room. They spoke in hushed tones, not so much because they were afraid the killer might hear their voices and realize they were different people but because they were both so nervous their mouths had gone completely dry.

They got ready for bed, putting on pajamas. Cindy kept jumping at every little sound, sure that someone was there in the shadows waiting to pounce. She kept reminding herself that it could be hours before the man showed, but that didn't help any. It only built anticipation which made her jump even harder every time she heard the house creaking.

She knew that Jeremiah was somewhere nearby. She kept fixating on that. It helped for the most part, but she found herself wishing she knew exactly how close by he was.

After an hour she finally made a trip to the restroom. She felt better as she stepped back into Sarah's room. The lights were out except for the faint glow of a nightlight near the floor to the left of the bed.

"Did you hear that noise a minute ago?" Candace asked, sounding freaked out.

"What noise?" Cindy whispered.

Suddenly, cold, hard steel touched the back of her neck.

20

Without thinking Cindy screamed. A hand clamped down on her mouth. She drove her foot down and back, driving her heel into the man's instep. She simultaneously rammed her elbow backward into his stomach. The hand on her mouth loosened. The gun barrel hit her in the back of the head, but it was a glancing blow. The pain was sharp, but she was still on her feet.

She spun away from him, moving to stand between him and Candace. Any second Jeremiah would be there and would protect them, but she would shield the girl for the moment. They didn't have to wait long. A dark shape loomed in the doorway. Her eyes strained to adjust to the low light in the room and she saw their rescuer twist their assailant's head. The killer's body slid to the floor with a thud.

"Is he dead?" she asked.

"Uh huh," came the garbled reply.

She leaped forward and threw her arms around her hero's neck and hugged him tight.

"Um, wrong guy. Please don't kiss me," she heard Martin say.

Cindy gasped and let go, jumping back.

Candace flipped on the light switch and stood there staring at both of them.

"Where's Jeremiah?" Cindy demanded.

"We agreed, after some strenuous debate, that he'd cover downstairs because of his injuries."

"What injuries?" Cindy demanded.

"From the fall backward on the stairs last night that I'm shocked didn't break his back," Martin said.

Cindy blinked. She knew Jeremiah had fought the man the night before. She didn't realize he'd been injured doing so.

Martin shook his head. "Don't worry about not knowing. He's good at hiding these things."

"He shouldn't be good at hiding them from me," Cindy muttered darkly.

Martin turned to Candace.

"Are you alright?" he asked her.

"Yes, but I was more scared than when I was getting chased by saboteurs in the park two Halloweens ago," she said.

"That sounds like an interesting story," Cindy said.

Cindy could hear the creak of a stair as someone walked up the staircase. She turned just as Jeremiah entered the room. He glanced down at the dead man on the floor and nodded.

"You can't blame that one on me," he said.

"Poor guy must have had some sort of attack. He died in my arms," Martin said. "It's a tragedy, really. And we came close to a second one."

"What?" Jeremiah asked.

"Apparently your fiancée has a type. She almost kissed me afterward," Martin said with a smirk.

"I did not!" Cindy exclaimed, feeling her cheeks turn red. "I thought he was you and I hugged him. That was it!"

"You hugged him?" Jeremiah asked.

"It was completely dark," Candace piped up, clearly trying to be helpful.

"You were hugging him in the dark in a bedroom?" Jeremiah asked.

"It wasn't like that! Martin, I'm going to kill you," she threatened.

"Not if my wife kills me first," he said.

"She'll have to get in line," Jeremiah said, his voice a low growl.

Cindy was feeling distressed until she noticed something. Usually when Jeremiah was stressed or upset his voice took on more of an accent. It hadn't, even though he'd sounded angry. She took a closer look at him and realized that he was struggling not to laugh.

"Both of you!" she shrieked, punching first Jeremiah in the shoulder then Martin. "Terrible!"

She stopped and glanced over at Candace. She took a deep breath and realized how surreal this must seem to the girl. She instantly felt bad about joking while there was the dead body of the man who would have murdered them on the floor.

"Are you okay?" she asked Candace.

"Yeah, I think so. It's just…weird. You deal with this a lot?"

"Unfortunately," Cindy said, nodding.

She walked over and hugged Candace.

"Don't kiss her either," Martin joked.

Cindy glared daggers at the agent even as she struggled not to giggle at that. There was something about the aftermath of terror when the endorphins released in your brain and you knew you were okay. It could make a person a bit giddy sometimes. It was like the most overwhelming sense of relief in the whole world and sometimes that was accompanied by laughter that on the face of it was wholly inappropriate.

"It's good to be alive," Martin said softly, as though reading her mind.

"Yes, it is," Cindy said.

~

Mark and Liam stood over the body for a moment before surveying the room. Everything had been over fifteen minutes earlier and they'd finally received the all clear to come in.

"How are we supposed to write this up? Act of Agency?" Mark grunted.

"It wouldn't be the first time," Liam said.

Jeremiah, Cindy, and Candace were downstairs in the living room with a couple of agents. Martin was upstairs with them, leaning against a wall, arms folded, watching the two detectives.

"I'll have my boss call your boss," Martin said. "That should help with the paperwork."

"In theory," Mark grumbled. "Do you guys even have paperwork?"

"Some of us."

"You?" Mark asked pointedly.

Martin shrugged noncommittally.

"Please tell me that this means you're leaving town now," Mark said.

"We go home on the second."

"Oh joy."

"I'll do my best to stay out of your hair."

"I would appreciate that."

"You're a good friend, Detective," Martin said.

"Excuse me?"

Martin rolled his eyes.

"To Jeremiah, I mean."

"Oh, thank you."

"He's really very lucky. Men like us don't have many friends, particularly those who know who we are and stick around anyway."

Mark thought about making a sarcastic comment but swallowed it. Martin was trying to be sincere. There was also something that for just a moment seemed wistful about the spy. It gave Mark pause.

"Are you lucky with your friends?" he asked.

Martin shook his head slowly.

"I'm sorry to hear that," Mark said. He was surprised to realize that he really meant that. Clearly, he was getting soft.

Martin pushed off the wall.

"I have somewhere I need to be. My associates downstairs can finish up. If you have any questions or need anything, just ask them," Martin said.

"Okay."

"Happy New Year, Gentlemen," Martin said.

"Same to you," Liam said.

"Happy New Year," Mark said, nodding to the man.

Martin turned and hurried down the stairs.

"How long do you think before we see him again?" Liam asked.

"With our luck? I'm sure he'll show up for Jeremiah and Cindy's wedding," Mark said.

"Something to look forward to."

Mark turned his attention to his partner.

"Speaking of weddings, have you figured out how you're going to ask Rebecca to marry you?"

"I've thought of several different scenarios."

"Like?"

"There are some special teas that open into flowers in hot water. I was thinking of trying to work with one of the local manufacturers to help me get her diamond ring inside one so it would appear in her cup."

"Nice, but tea is her livelihood, not her hobby," Mark pointed out.

"That's exactly the conclusion I came to."

"What else have you got?"

"Well, there are the standards, fancy dinner, ring in the champagne glass."

"Again with ring in the beverage."

"Yeah," Liam said. "I wasn't really feeling that. I mean, I decided if I was going to put it in a glass, I'd first freeze it in an ice cube."

"Make her work for it? That's just cruel."

"Yeah. Plus, let's be honest, I'd be even more impatient than her."

Mark laughed at that. He had a crazy mental image of Liam sitting there screaming at a cube of ice to melt faster.

"So, what is the winner?" Mark asked as he bent down to get a closer look at the dead man."

"When she was little her uncle used to create elaborate scavenger hunts for her on her birthday and she had to follow the clues to get her present. She still loves puzzles and those kinds of things."

"So, you're going to do a New Year's Eve scavenger hunt proposal?" Mark asked.

Liam nodded.

"Now that is cool," Mark said approvingly. "That's the kind of thing you guys will talk about for years to come."

"I hope so," Liam said.

"You will. She'd be crazy not to say yes."

"Thanks."

Liam looked on edge.

"What's wrong? Worried that she won't?"

"A little, but that's not the real problem."

"What is it?" Mark asked.

Liam indicated the body on the ground. "This fire is out, but we've only got a couple of days left to deal with the other one.

He was right. They had stopped this killer, but they still had work to do. They had to save Geanie.

~

That night Cindy invited Kyle and Bunni to join the rest of them at Joseph and Geanie's house where Joseph cooked one of his gourmet dinners. The talk around the dinner table was alternately playful and solemn as they each thought about the events of the past few days and what was ahead of them.

They finally adjourned into the living room afterward. After discussing how filming was just about wrapped up for Kyle and Bunni at The Zone things finally turned serious.

"We've solved one crisis. That just leaves one more," Joseph said grimly.

He was only voicing what Cindy and the others were thinking.

"What's that?" Kyle asked.

She had forgotten briefly that he and Bunni weren't part of their everyday lives. That in itself was kind of a miracle. It really showed how much Kyle's and her relationship had evolved over the last few months. He even seemed to be making a real effort to get along with Jeremiah. She was grateful for that even if she didn't entirely trust it yet. She realized she kept mentally waiting for the other shoe to drop in that regard. She also really liked Bunni and was hoping that Kyle would wake up and realize that she was the perfect girl for him sooner rather than later.

Cindy briefly filled Kyle and Bunni in on the whole secret society wanting Joseph to kill Geanie thing. She ended with the fact that he was supposed to do so by midnight on New Year's Eve.

"That's insane," Bunni said.

"I know, right?" Cindy said.

"We have to do something, and we don't have much time," Joseph said, agitated.

"You don't have a plan?" Bunni asked.

"No," Cindy said.

"But won't there be consequences if New Year's Eve comes and goes and she isn't dead?"

"I guess I'm going to have to deal with those. We've run out of time to catch these guys. New Year's Eve is almost here and it's not like we can just kill her," Joseph said.

There was a moment of silence and then suddenly Kyle jumped to his feet.

"We can totally kill Geanie!"

21

Everyone turned to stare at Kyle.

"Um no, we can't," Joseph said.

"No, no, hear me out," Kyle said. "We have access to some of the best makeup artists and stunt people in the industry. We can fake kill her and make it seem completely real."

"No!" Cindy snapped.

Jeremiah reached out and squeezed her hand. He gave her a knowing look. It was clear to her that he could tell that she was thinking about his faked death when they were in Israel. She still had nightmares about that alley, the gunshots, and seeing Jeremiah apparently dead.

"We'll all know she's okay," he said softly.

Her throat tightened a bit, but she nodded.

"What did you have in mind?" Geanie asked Kyle.

"Movies and television are all about make believe, about making things look real even when they're not."

"You mean you didn't really go over Niagara Falls in a boat?" Mark said sarcastically.

Kyle rolled his eyes. "Please it was a completely different waterfall. I'm a daredevil, not an idiot."

Cindy had oftentimes thought those two things one and the same, but she held her tongue.

"Hold it. We've got several problems as I see it," Joseph said.

"You've got to fake kill Geanie," Bunni said.

"And you have to do it in such a way that whoever might be watching truly believes you killed her," Cindy added.

"But since this is all ostensibly an initiation to get into this secret society, you can't do it in a way that the police could ever pin the blame on you," Mark said.

"But one of the draws of this group is that they do help people cover up such things," Joseph pointed out with a frown.

"Yes, but they can't risk people who aren't even members yet botching things so badly that it's hard to cover up. I mean, the killers in this case are all people with some measure of stature or wealth or something to lose. These aren't run of the mill, average guys," Kyle said.

"And besides, someone could agree to cut a deal for leniency in exchange for exposing the group," Mark pointed out.

"Wait a minute," Cindy said, as thoughts raced through her mind. She felt like there was something right in front of her that she should be seeing, but she wasn't. "Why hasn't someone done that already?"

There was silence for a moment as everyone let that sink in.

"Maybe no one's been caught," Bunni finally suggested.

"Or if they were, the society swept it under the rug, took care of it?" Kyle suggested.

"Or took care of them," Jeremiah said darkly.

"The only way to make sure someone doesn't talk is to silence them," Mark said, nodding.

"So, have there been any high profile murders where the suspected murderer ended up dead as well?" Cindy asked.

Geanie shook her head. "They wouldn't necessarily be high profile murders. Think about your former boss and his friend. Neither of them were in the public eye when they killed to try and get into this club."

"True, but they were both ambitious, up and comers," Joseph pointed out.

"They were still low enough on the food chain that they didn't have the entire world to lose by trusting the society to do something for them," Kyle said. "Someone like Joseph, now he'd have everything to lose by getting caught and no real incentive to trust the society to help him out."

"I've seen Joseph's lawyers at work. Joseph could stand up in the middle of church, stab Geanie through the heart with a knife he bought the day before, and he'd still stand a 50-50 chance of acquittal. He'd be better off relying on his own team instead of some mystery group he doesn't know and hasn't seen in action," Mark said.

"Thanks, Mark. I feel so much better," Geanie said, glaring at him.

"Not that he would, obviously, because, you know, the love and everything," Mark said.

"Yes, because if it weren't for the love and everything I'd totally do that just for fun," Joseph said sarcastically.

Mark rolled his eyes. "I'm not saying you'd ever kill anyone, just that if you did you'd stand a decent chance of getting away with it."

"Good to know," Joseph said.

"So, no one piss off Joseph," Kyle joked.

"Okay, look," Traci said, speaking up for the first time. "How do we stage it so that it appears like Joseph had nothing to do with killing Geanie, but this secret society will believe he did?"

"Car accident," Jeremiah said softly. "That's the best way to disguise a murder. Well, the best way for most people."

"How would you do it?" Mark asked bluntly.

"There are untraceable toxins that can simulate all kinds of natural ailments."

"Like the Green Pastures board member, Dr. Tanner?" Cindy asked.

Jeremiah shook his head. "The autopsy turned up the poison that caused the heart attack in his case. It was sloppy work."

A chill passed over Cindy. Even though she knew who Jeremiah was and what he'd done when he worked for the Mossad, every once in a while there was a moment where it just hit her harder.

There were several seconds of uncomfortable silence as everyone stared at Jeremiah.

"Relax, I've no plans to kill any of you," he finally said with an exaggerated sigh.

"Sure, you're not *planning* on it," Mark said.

Kyle shifted uncomfortably in his chair and cleared his throat.

"Anyway, car crash, that's definitely something we can help fake," Kyle said.

"Absolutely," Bunni said with an enthusiastic nod.

"Unfortunately, it means trashing a car," Kyle said with a grimace.

"A small price to pay," Joseph said with a shrug. "Besides, someone's birthday is coming up and I think a new car is in order anyway."

Geanie looked at him with wide eyes. "New car? What?"

"I'm not telling you," he said, looking at her like she had lost her mind.

"Doesn't the condemned woman get a last request?" Geanie asked.

"That's not funny," Joseph muttered, his skin growing pale.

"Sorry," Geanie said, dropping her eyes.

"Anyway, we've got one more problem that we haven't addressed," Joseph said.

"What's that?" Cindy asked.

"In order for this to work and for them to get the message that I ... killed... her, then the car crash has to be made public."

"Which means everyone is going to think I'm dead," Geanie said.

"We would be devastating a lot of people, putting them through that grief," Cindy said. "And we don't know if it will be an hour or a week before the society contacts Joseph."

"And we couldn't trust anyone outside this room to be able to play along," Mark said grimly. "This is a bad plan."

"It's the only plan," Kyle said. "Unless you have some other way you think you can contact these guys."

"I have to agree with Kyle," Jeremiah said. "It's our only move."

"Thank you," Kyle said appreciatively.

"Do you think any of the guys that we know are involved would actually talk?" Bunni said.

"Like Ken, the guy who killed his secretary?" Mark asked.

"Yes."

"No, that guy is still hoping to get off clean. I heard his lawyer's trying to make out that Ivan actually killed her like he killed the other girl. He's not worried enough to try and cut a deal. Besides, I'm not sure he had any point of contact with the group besides Ivan."

"When you had Joseph get approached by Ivan at that charity event, wasn't Ivan supposed to have some other friends there?" Cindy asked.

"Yeah, that guy Gareth who kept schmoozing Ivan said so," Mark said.

"So, maybe there is more than one member of the society here in California," Cindy said.

"Okay, maybe. All we need to do is figure out which one of the rich and powerful people at that event had something to hide," Mark said sarcastically.

"At least we know one thing. Any member of the society had to kill a woman to gain entrance and the society would help them cover it up or at least redirect blame," Geanie said.

And just like that something that had been gnawing at the back of Cindy's brain sprang forth.

"Jason Todd!" she blurted out.

"Who?" Bunni asked.

"He's a computer guy, millionaire, who killed his wife. I was on the jury, but things went sideways," Cindy said. "He had the most evil looking eyes. What if he killed his wife as his initiation?"

Mark nodded. "That would explain why despite all the evidence and everyone's best efforts they haven't been able to make it through a single trial yet. And we still never found out who hired the assassin to tamper with the jury."

"But we know that the goal was to set Jason Todd free so that he could be killed," Cindy said. "Would the society want to kill one of its members?"

"It would if they thought he might be persuaded to talk," Joseph said.

Mark stood up abruptly.

"What's wrong?" Jeremiah asked.

"I'm going to make a few phone calls. We need to have a talk with Jason Todd."

~

Six hours later Mark and Liam were sitting across a table from Jason Todd. The last several months had not been kind to the millionaire who looked thin and haggard.

"I won't answer any questions without my attorney Sebastian Morris," Jason said before they could say a word to him.

"He's been notified and he's on his way," Mark said. "I have to admit he's a good attorney. How did you find him?"

"He came highly recommended," Jason said, narrowing his eyes and clearly trying to figure out what Mark's angle was.

"The problem with trials is that no matter how good your attorney, you're still gambling on what twelve people are going to decide, and people are emotional, irrational and easily swayed by a compelling narrative."

Jason just shrugged.

"But, of course, given how good your attorney is he would have already warned you about that and told you that your safest move would be to strike a deal, particularly if you had information that was valuable."

Jason tilted his head slightly, and Mark knew he had the man's attention.

"D.A. wasn't interested in what I had to say."

"Who told you that?" Liam asked.

"Sebastian."

Mark and Liam exchanged looks.

"What?" Jason asked.

"I talked to the D.A. a couple of hours ago. Sebastian never approached him about a deal," Mark said.

"You're lying," Jason hissed.

"He's not," Liam said.

"Given how long this has been dragging out and the disruptions it's been causing they'd love to come to some sort of arrangement if you had anything to offer that would help them."

"I want my attorney," Jason said.

"Did your attorney tell you the details of what happened during the Pine Springs trial?" Liam asked.

"Yeah, he told me a crazy reporter infiltrated the jury pool and a gambler was trying to get the inside track for some Vegas boss who was taking wagers on the outcome."

"We're the cops who caught those guys," Mark said.

Jason looked uncertain of what to say in response.

"But it sounds like your attorney left out the most important part. Someone murdered a prospective juror, took his place, and was doing everything he could to get you set free."

"Seriously?" Jason asked, clearly startled.

"Seriously."

"I guess I've got friends I don't know about," Jason muttered.

"He was trying to free you in order to kill you. You don't have friends, you have enemies," Mark said.

"And we think you already knew about them," Liam added.

"Who hired the guy to kill me?" Jason asked.

Mark leaned forward and narrowed his eyes. "We think you know."

The door opened and Sebastian Morris entered, looking just as slick and smarmy as Mark remembered. He scowled at Mark and Liam.

"Detectives, I protest-"

"Liar!" Jason screamed as he leaped up from the table and lunged at Sebastian.

22

Mark and Liam jumped up and grabbed hold of Jason. He had his hands wrapped around his attorney's throat and was screaming incoherently. They wrestled him off Sebastian and slammed him back down into his seat.

"Guard!" Mark shouted.

Moments later Jason was handcuffed to the table. He was still shouting angrily at Sebastian. The guard stepped back, but did not leave the room.

"Quiet!" Liam said, his voice filling the room, startling even Mark who turned to glance at his partner.

"I don't know what you've been telling my client to cause this outburst," Sebastian said.

"I'm not your client anymore. You're fired!" Jason shouted.

"Please, let's just settle down. You're not thinking clearly," Sebastian said, regaining his composure.

"Oh, I'm thinking clear and seeing clear for the first time. You're working for them," Jason said.

"Them who?" Mark pressed.

"No one," Sebastian said quickly. "My client is suffering from persecution delusions given the trauma that he's experienced at the hands of law enforcement and the irresponsible media coverage of his family tragedy. He's not always rational."

"Then how come you haven't ever tried to enter psychological evaluations into the record?" Mark asked.

"Because it sounds like you're calling him crazy and if he is then that changes things considerably," Liam added.

"I'm not crazy," Jason said emphatically. He turned to look at Mark and Liam. "Detectives, I want a new attorney and I want to turn state's evidence. I didn't murder my wife, but I know who did."

"He's not thinking clearly," Sebastian said.

"I'm sorry, but you're not his attorney. He fired you, so you no longer have the right to be here," Mark said.

He saw fear in Sebastian's eyes, and it made him smile.

"Guard, please remove Mr. Morris," Liam said.

The guard nodded and put a hand on Sebastian's arm. Sebastian shook it off angrily. He looked down at Jason malevolently.

"You'll regret this," Sebastian said.

"On the contrary, this is the first thing I've done right since this whole mess started," Jason said.

The guard left with Sebastian. As soon as the door had closed behind them Mark and Liam sat down again.

"Now, tell us who killed your wife," Mark said.

"They call themselves Dominos Orbis Terrarium Fecit, Masters of the World."

Mark felt a thrill of excitement. Cindy was right. And now they had a name to put to the shadowy organization.

"A secret society?" Mark asked, struggling to keep the excitement out of his voice.

"Yes. They cater to the wealthy and the powerful, offering things money can't buy."

"And they approached you to join?" Liam asked.

"They did," Jason said. "But I didn't like the cost."

"They wanted you to kill your wife?" Mark asked.

"Yes," Jason said, slightly surprised.

"And you didn't want to?" Liam pushed.

"No!"

"Even though she was terrified of you and thinking of divorcing you?" Mark asked.

"No! Look, we had our problems. I have problems. I'm not a nice guy. I've done a lot of bad things, but I'd never kill her. And I had no idea she was thinking of divorcing me. I mean, look. Yes, things were rough sometimes between us. And sometimes they got physical, but it went both ways. My wife grew up on the streets. She never wanted to go back there. I had no illusions. I knew she married me primarily for my money, but I loved her. She signed a prenup. She knew if she divorced me she'd get nothing. So, I don't buy that crap that she was looking for a divorce. It doesn't make sense."

Mark glanced at Liam and could tell that his partner was thinking just as hard as he was about what Jason was telling them. Something wasn't adding up. Cassidy Todd's best friend had testified that she'd changed her mind about divorce just a couple of days before she was murdered. A divorce attorney had said the same thing. What if they were both lying?

"Why would the secret society kill your wife?" Mark asked.

"I got the feeling that turning them down was not an option. They were pretty pissed when I did. The first couple weeks I had no idea what was going on, who would want to kill her. Then I had time to think about it and I realized they must have framed me for killing her to punish me. I kept thinking it was a stupid mistake on their part. I would have kept my mouth shut about the society if they'd left me alone after I said no. But killing my wife and framing me? I've been trying to get someone to listen, to tell them what I know."

"But your attorney was blocking you," Mark said. "Who recommended him?"

Jason blanched.

"Was it one of the Masters of the World?" Liam asked.

"I didn't think about it. It was a colleague, Jeff Watson. I saw him talking to one of the guys trying to recruit me at a party I had. I thought they were just talking sports, hunting or something."

"Who were the guys trying to recruit you?" Mark asked intently.

They were close to getting enough information to help take down the society or, at the very least, to help them protect Joseph and Geanie. Because in the back of his mind it kept playing over and over that if Joseph didn't kill Geanie the society would.

"There was Pierre, a French financier from back east somewhere. I never got a last name. I only met him once. Most of my contact was with Roman Juarez, he's an independent filmmaker. We knew each other from college."

"We need to know everything you can remember about your interactions with both of them," Mark said.

~

An hour later Mark and Liam were in the car heading back to Pine Springs. Jason had given them a lot of good information and it was clear he was willing to testify

219

regarding what he knew about the society. They also had four names: Jeff Watson, Roman Juarez, Pierre, and the lawyer Sebastian Morris. The lawyer might be a member of the society or he might just work for them. Either way they needed to try and crack him which wasn't going to be easy.

"There's something not right here," Liam said.

"You got that, too?" Mark asked.

"Yeah. If the society wanted to punish or silence Jason for turning them down, they wouldn't frame him for murder. That's just asking for him to strike a deal to sell them out. And if his lawyer really was working for the society then what was the point? Keep him from ratting them all out? If so, why work so hard to have him set free? Someone wanted him dead and hired the assassin to rig the jury and make sure he got off. I mean, that could have easily been the attorney, but why frame Jason to set him free to kill him?"

"To cause confusion?" Mark said.

"If so, it worked."

Mark took a deep breath. "Maybe we're looking at this all wrong. Maybe they sent in the lawyer to get him off before they realized he was going to be a problem."

"What do you mean?"

"What if the wife gets killed and the society thinks Jason did it, that he changed his mind? They'd then put in motion their machine to help him beat the charge, which would include a shark of an attorney like Sebastian."

"But then Sebastian realizes Jason's going to try and out the secret society and blame them for the murder?" Liam asked.

"Yeah."

"So, the Masters think Jason killed Cassidy and Jason thinks the Masters killed Cassidy."

"But what if there's a third option?" Mark said. "What if someone else killed her?"

"Why?"

"I don't know, but I think we should try and find out who else might have wanted her dead."

"Is it just me or is this whole thing way too convoluted?" Liam asked.

"It's not you," Mark muttered.

"Oh good. That makes me feel loads better."

"Glad I could help."

"So, we need to get background on Watson and Juarez," Liam said.

"While we're at it, let's run our lawyer friend as well."

"And we need to talk to the detectives on the Todd case and see if they ever investigated anyone besides Jason for his wife's murder."

"With any luck they did, but I'm not holding my breath," Mark said.

"Me neither. So that I'm clear, what is our goal?"

"Get someone to crack so we can put an end to the Masters before we have to fake Geanie's death."

Liam snorted.

"What? You don't think we can do that in two days?"

"I don't think we can do that in two years. Ivan died before giving up the society and he was a new member. Even if we manage to say capture a dozen of them the society will still go on. We'd have to capture all its members to shut it down and that's just not going to happen. Some of these guys will be so shrouded that only a couple of people will even know who they are."

"Your optimism is really warming my heart," Mark growled.

"I'm serious, these things are insidious. In a lot of ways they're worse than the mafia."

Again Mark got that tickle in the back of his mind that warned him that Liam's knowledge about the mafia wasn't just academic.

"Well, we can at least try to get enough of them that they forget about hassling Joseph."

"That is an achievable goal. They'll shut down recruiting while they figure out how bad the damage is."

"I wish we knew who the other two invitees to this little party are," Mark said.

"And whether or not they've already paid their entrance dues?"

"Yeah. I just can't shake the feeling that there's two women somewhere out there that we won't be able to save."

"Let's focus on the one we can," Liam said.

Mark nodded.

"Losing Geanie is not an option."

Mark fixated on that thought while Liam called in and requested background information on their three suspects. He wished he had a last name to go along with the fourth, Pierre, but hopefully they could eventually get that from one of the other three.

His mind was also turning over and over the problem of who killed Cassidy Todd and framed Jason. It was the least pressing problem he had, but solving a homicide was much more in his wheelhouse than dealing with secret societies and ritual murder. One thing was certain, whoever had done it had done a neat job of setting up Jason to take the fall. Then again, it sounded like the millionaire had done a lot of the heavy lifting on that himself. Someone else just stepped in and took advantage of the situation. Someone who knew the next door neighbor would be watching and listening.

"What? Say that again?" Liam said.

Mark glanced at his partner. The other detective was gripping his phone tight and had a look of consternation on his face.

"You're sure? How?"

Something had happened and from the look on Liam's face Mark would wager that it was bad. He could feel himself tensing up as he waited for the bad news. He didn't interrupt, waiting instead for Liam to get all the information.

"Keep us advised," Liam said before hanging up.

"Problem?" Mark asked.

"A big one."

"Well? What's going on?" Mark asked.

Liam took a deep breath.

"Jason Todd is dead."

23

"What!" Mark blurted out.

"Someone stabbed him."

"Who?"

"They don't know."

Mark swore.

"How is that possible?" Mark demanded.

Liam didn't answer.

"This has gone too far," Mark said.

"I have a feeling the worst is yet to come," Liam said.

Mark had a sinking suspicion that his partner was right.

"We need to run background on the names we have," Mark said.

"I've already got Wendell on it," Liam said. "I asked him to do a deep dive so it's going to take some time."

"And meanwhile we're just stuck waiting."

"There has to be something we can do," Liam said.

"There is. We need to try to get Kenneth Cartwright to talk," Mark said.

"We don't know that he ever knew anyone else in the society besides Ivan."

"Yeah, well we're going to shake everything he does know out of him," Mark growled.

~

Cindy stood next to Geanie watching in fascinated horror as stunt guys from Kyle's film crew monkeyed with Geanie's car.

"This is insane," Cindy whispered.

"Tell me about it," Geanie said. "What kind of car do you think Joseph is getting me for my birthday?" she asked a few seconds later.

Cindy chuckled. "A better one than this."

It was true. Having money hadn't changed Geanie all that much at her core. To Cindy the funniest part was that Geanie was still driving the same car that she'd had when they met. It wasn't exactly a hunk of junk, but neither was it a nice car. It was getting up there mileage wise, and it was high time she did have a new car.

"I'm serious! What do you think it will be? Maybe a new Mustang," Geanie said, looking excited.

"Your husband could buy you a dozen Lamborghinis and not even blink and your go-to thought is a new Mustang?" Cindy asked disbelievingly. "Maybe he might get me a Mustang, which I would love, but I think he's probably aiming on the more expensive side for you."

"Yeah, but would I really want to drive a Lamborghini to the grocery store?" Geanie asked.

"If you had insurance? Yes," Cindy said emphatically.

It was a surreal conversation but somehow, that was appropriate given what they were watching.

"You know, if we really wanted to do this right, we'd need a body, a Jane Doe," one of the guys was saying to his friends.

"No, no, no. What we really need is a fire that burns hot enough that it wouldn't leave a body behind. No corpse required," a second guy said.

"This is a morbid conversation," Cindy muttered.

"Are you sure these are stunt guys and not some shady underworld figures?" Geanie asked.

"Well, Kyle works with them," Cindy said.

"That didn't answer my question."

"Hey, how long have you guys been stuntmen?" Cindy called out.

The first guy was quick to respond.

"Mitch here has been a stuntman for fifteen years. Coop, twelve, and I've been working in the industry since I was six."

"Since you were six?" Geanie asked incredulously.

"Kids need stunt doubles, too," he said with a toothy grin. "You ladies are in good hands. We're going to blow up this car real good."

He turned back to the car and dove under the hood.

"Does that guy scare you?" Cindy whispered.

"Little bit."

The front door of the mansion opened and Joseph walked out with Kyle and Lizzie.

"How's it going out here?" Joseph asked.

"They're going to blow up my car," Geanie said, sounding a bit distraught. "And I'm afraid they're going to blow me up with it."

"No, don't worry about that," Kyle said enthusiastically. "They'll run the car on remote control. No one will be in it when it crashes."

"Okay, won't that be obvious, though?" Cindy asked.

Kyle shook his head. "We control the spin, remember? And we're working with local law enforcement. Whatever we say happened will be the official word while we try to catch these psychos."

"You're enjoying this, aren't you?" Cindy said.

"Yes! I get to use my skills and people to help you solve one of your mysteries," Kyle said. "I think it's awesome."

She bit her lip. Awesome wasn't exactly the word she would have chosen, but she didn't want to discourage him.

Coop came over to them, looking very pleased with himself.

"How's it going?" Kyle asked.

"Really good," Coop said, wiping his hands on a rag.

Cindy noticed that while Coop was talking to Kyle, he was staring directly at Lizzie.

"Kyle, bro, I don't think you've introduced us," Coop said.

"Oh, I'm sorry," Kyle said. "This is Joseph, he owns the place. And this is his wife, Geanie, whose car this is."

Just when she thought her brother couldn't be more blind when it came to these things, he totally missed the point.

Cindy picked up the slack. "Coop, may I introduce you to Miss Lizzie Matthews? Lizzie, this is Coop," she said, not knowing the rest of his name.

"Cooper," he said, holding out his hand.

"It's nice to meet you, Cooper," Lizzie said, flushing slightly as she shook his hand.

"Where's Jeremiah?" Geanie asked.

"He's counseling Traci," Lizzie said, without taking her eyes off Cooper. "I think what you do is fascinating," she told him.

"Thank you, miss. I'd be happy to tell you more about it, maybe over dinner sometime."

Lizzie nodded. "I'd like that."

Cindy smiled. At least one sister was having a good day. That was good. It had been clear to everyone that Traci was in rough shape. She really hoped Jeremiah could help her.

"Maybe in a little bit we should go in and pray with Traci," Geanie suggested.

"That's a great idea," Cindy said.

A gas jet went off next to the car and fire leaped fifteen feet in the air.

"Whoa, that's awesome!" Lizzie said, sounding a bit awestruck.

"I think we could all use some extra prayer," Cindy added.

~

Jeremiah was sitting with Traci in the dining room. It wasn't the most comfortable place to talk, but he didn't want it to be a room she was familiar with and spent much time in.

"How are you doing?" he asked gently.

She smiled at him. "Not good," she said, her words in clear opposition to her expression.

"It's good that you can admit that," he said.

"I'm scared all the time," she admitted.

"It's understandable, given what you've been through."

"I don't like feeling this way."

"No one does."

"I need to not feel this way," she said, still smiling.

"Well, I'm going to help you work on that," he said gently. "It won't be easy, but eventually you'll get through this."

~

Mark and Liam sat down across the table from Kenneth Cartwright who looked supremely unconcerned at their appearance. He was drinking a cup of water when they came in and he finished it slowly before putting the cup down on the table. His nonchalance irked Mark who had the almost overwhelming urge to smack the smug, confident look right off Cartwright's face.

"I have nothing to say without my lawyer present," Cartwright said.

"You know Jason Todd said the same thing a couple of hours ago right before he told us everything he knew about the Masters of the World," Mark said.

"Who?" Cartwright asked, hesitating just a moment too long before asking.

"Jason Todd, another candidate for entry into the secret society you and Ivan were trying to get into. You remember the one, Masters of the World they call themselves," Liam said.

"I'm afraid I don't know what you're talking about," Cartwright said.

Mark slammed his hand down on the table hard enough to make the prisoner jump.

"Don't play with us. We're the only ones who can protect you from the Masters. They don't take kindly to snitches," Mark said.

"I'm no snitch!" Kenneth denied hotly.

Mark smiled. "That's not what they heard."

Kenneth actually jerked and his hands started shaking.

"They think I talked?" he asked.

Mark was pleased that he'd managed to rattle Kenneth enough that the man wasn't even bothering to deny the group existed or that he'd been attempting to join.

"You know what they do to people who talk?" Liam asked.

"But I haven't said anything!" Kenneth protested.

"Doesn't matter that you didn't. The only thing that's going to help you now, though, is us," Liam said.

"And we only help scum like you when we're feeling charitable," Mark said.

"So, give us a reason to feel charitable," Liam said.

Cartwright was panicking. He was sweating and his hands were shaking even harder. Whatever he knew of the secret society, he knew enough to realize he was in trouble if they thought he was talking.

"You have to protect me. These guys are killers," Cartwright said.

"So are you," Liam pointed out.

"All I did was kill one person."

Mark blinked in surprise. He hadn't expected Cartwright to confess to that.

"Your secretary, Rose Meyer," Mark prompted.

"Yes, stupid girl was going to ruin my entire life. She just wouldn't keep her mouth shut," Cartwright said.

"So, you thought why not kill two birds with one stone. Get rid of her and get yourself invited into the Masters of the World," Mark said.

"Yes, but you don't understand. These guys are monsters. The things they'll do… I warned Ivan, but he insisted, said it would be good for us. He said the society would take us to the next level, help us become rich and powerful beyond our dreams. I knew there was going to be a cost."

Mark couldn't believe what he was hearing. Cartwright sounded like he had actually not wanted to join because of what he'd found out.

"Give us a name," Mark said. "Who recruited Ivan?"

"I don't know his name. He just told me it was some rich French guy."

"Who else?" Mark demanded.

"I don't know! That was it."

"Then how do you know they're monsters?" Liam asked.

"There weren't any names, but he told me about some of the things they did, some of the atrocities they committed and got away with. They manipulate so many things. We think we have free will, but we don't!"

Cartwright was raving and his entire body was shaking. Sweat was pouring off him.

Something's wrong, Mark thought. Alarm bells were going off in his head.

"Let's just calm down," Mark said. "Are you alright?"

Cartwright was still ranting but it had grown incoherent. Flecks of foam appeared at the corner of his mouth. He suddenly began to convulse.

Both Mark and Liam jumped to their feet.

Mark pounded on the door and shouted, "We need a doctor!"

Cartwright fell onto the floor as a guard opened the door.

"What's going-" the guard stopped mid-sentence as he took in the scene. He grabbed his radio. "We need a doctor in interrogation 4. Prisoner is convulsing."

Cartwright let out an agonizing scream that cut off abruptly. His entire body went slack.

Mark started to move forward, ready to check for a pulse and start performing CPR if necessary. Liam grabbed him around the chest, though, pulling him back.

"We have to help him!" Mark said.

Liam shook his head fiercely.

"Don't touch him," Liam warned. "I think he's been poisoned."

24

Ten minutes later it was all over. Kenneth Cartwright was dead.

Mark just sat there, staring into space, struggling to process everything that had happened.

"I think we've been played," Liam said quietly.

"You think this was about us?" Mark asked.

"Both these guys have been alive for months waiting trial. The day we decide to visit they're both killed. I think the new element was us."

"Or the fact that we outed the lawyer's real role in all this."

"We need to be on our toes," Liam advised. "Who knows what will happen next."

~

Three hours later Mark and Liam were finally free to leave. They started driving back to Joseph and Geanie's house.

"What are we going to tell them?" Liam finally asked.

"The truth."

Mark's phone rang and he answered it.

"Hello?"

"Detective Walters?"

"Yes."

"This is Detective Griffin. I just caught what looks like a suicide and I'm going to have a few questions for you. Apparently, you witnessed an altercation earlier today between my vic and another man."

"I did?" Mark asked.

"Yes. Obviously, this can wait until the second at this point. I'm fairly certain you won't be able to shed any light on my investigation. I just wanted to touch base. Being the holidays, I know you've got better things to do. And, to be blunt, so do I. In the unlikely scenario that this wasn't a suicide, I've got a list as long as my arm of people that might have wanted this guy dead and not a single person who will care that he's gone as far as I can tell."

"Okay, sure, the second will be fine. I'll help however I can," Mark said.

"I appreciate that."

"Just one thing? Who's the victim?"

"A lawyer by the name of Sebastian Morris. He ate a bullet about two hours ago."

"Okay, thanks," Mark managed to say. "Talk to you in a couple of days."

"What is it?" Liam asked.

"Sebastian was shot in the head two hours ago. They think it's a suicide but are just doing follow up."

"What does that mean?"

"The society is cleaning house," Mark muttered.

"What does this mean for Geanie and Joseph?"

"I wish I knew. We need to get to their house. Now."

~

Jeremiah and Cindy were listening as Kyle told them his plans for spring. They were in Geanie and Joseph's living room along with several others including the stuntmen, Traci, Lizzie, Geanie, Joseph, Bunni, Candace, Josh, and Becca.

"Say that again?" Cindy asked.

"The owner of the Escape! Channel, RLS, just announced that we're going to be filming several episodes in Prague. It's so exciting," Kyle said.

"Usually we don't get to go somewhere so glamorous," Bunni added.

"That's a very romantic city," Joseph said.

"I'm counting on it," Bunni said, blushing as she glanced toward Kyle.

"Are you guys going to be in town tomorrow night for New Year's Eve?" Josh asked.

"No, we've got to hop a plane tonight," Kyle said. "I wish we didn't. The boss called. He needs us to start filming on the first."

"That's insane," Cindy said.

"It is what it is," Kyle said with a shrug. "I'm just upset I'm not going to be here to see everything get resolved."

"We'll make sure to keep you in the loop," Cindy said.

"What about the rest of you, do you have plans for tomorrow night?" Candace asked.

Jeremiah winced. They might, depending on how things went with Mark and Liam's investigation into the secret society. He was actually surprised that they had been gone pretty much all day and that they hadn't checked in yet.

"Hopefully not," Joseph said.

"I promised I'd go back to my other sister's house in the morning so I could help with the kids tomorrow night," Lizzie said, looking apologetically at Traci.

Traci reached out and hugged her.

"I'm just glad you could be here when you were," Traci said.

"Well, for those of you who can come, we'd like to invite you to a New Year's Eve party tomorrow night at The Zone," Josh said.

"Is this the one you have at The Top of the World restaurant at the hotel next to the park?" Joseph asked hesitantly.

"No, but would you like to go to that one?" Josh asked.

"No!" Joseph said. "I was there a few months ago under less than pleasant circumstances."

It was when he'd been undercover talking about the secret society. Jeremiah didn't blame him for not wanting to repeat that experience. Jeremiah and Cindy also had less than fond memories of the whole place thanks to her experiences being sequestered in the hotel during jury duty.

"Okay, cool. Then I'd like to invite you to a different gathering. It's at Boone's in the park. It's much smaller, mostly family and friends."

Jeremiah glanced around and one by one everyone who wasn't going out of town nodded.

"We'll be there," Jeremiah said.

"It's been a rough year. I think we all need a chance to celebrate seeing the old year die," Joseph said.

"Particularly if none of us has died," Geanie added.

"Yes," Cindy said emphatically. "I have to go in for a half day tomorrow, but I'm free after that."

"I need to do some work in the morning as well," Jeremiah said.

If I'm not needed here, he thought.

Joseph's phone rang. He pulled it out of his pocket and answered it. As soon as he did, he went white as a sheet. He quickly put the phone on speaker.

"The auditions will not be held this year. The society is focusing on other priorities at the moment," an electronically disguised voice said. "Should we start to actively recruit again we will be in touch."

Before Joseph could respond the mystery caller hung up.

They all sat for a moment in stunned silence.

"Thank you, God," Cindy said, her eyes closed as she prayed, repeating the words several times.

"Well that was unexpected," Kyle said after a few moments.

"I don't know what happened, but I'm so grateful," Joseph said.

"Here's to hoping they lose your number permanently," Cindy said.

"Amen," Geanie and Traci whispered together.

"This is it. We're free," Joseph said.

"No need to fake my death," Geanie said, tears of relief in her eyes.

"Well, on that note, I think it's time to go," Kyle said.

He stood up and everyone else followed suit.

~

"Three more minutes and we're there," Liam said as they neared the turn for the hill that Joseph's house was on.

Mark's thoughts were racing ahead to what he was going to tell everyone once they got there. A sick knot twisted itself around in his stomach. It had been a bad year and the last thing they needed was for it to end with a bang.

~

Everyone walked outside to say goodbyes. Kyle hugged first Cindy then Jeremiah. This time he was prepared for the gesture and hugged him back. People lingered by their cars for a moment, especially Bunni who looked especially sad as she was saying goodbye to everyone.

In the distance Jeremiah could hear a car engine. It sounded like it was coming up the hill. He hoped it was Mark and Liam.

Suddenly there was the faintest hint of gas in the air. Jeremiah turned toward Geanie's car just as it exploded in a fireball. The hood flew straight up in the air, twisted and then crashed back down on the car's roof.

Everyone stopped and stared, dumbstruck. Twenty seconds later the car was nothing but a steaming husk of charred and twisted metal.

"Alright!" Coop shouted.

"Wow," Lizzie said, her eyes bright with excitement and wonder.

"Happy New Year!" yelled Mitch.

Geanie looked absolutely stricken.

"Wooweee, couldn't let a good explosion like that go to waste," the third stuntman said admiringly. "Wasn't that something?"

Mark and Liam's car rocketed into view and Liam brought the car to a skidding stop not far from the wreckage. They both scrambled out of their car and stood, staring at the burning one.

"What is happening?" Mark roared.

"Fireworks, apparently," Jeremiah said.

It was an appropriate end to an explosive year filled with unforeseen events. He took a deep breath as he tried to let it all go.

"Honey?" Joseph said, looking as shocked as the rest of them.

"Yeah?" Geanie asked.

"I hadn't decided yet. Mustang or Lamborghini?"

Geanie looked incapable of actually making a decision. Fortunately, she didn't have to.

"She'll take one of each," Cindy said quickly. "One for the grocery store and the other for fun."

"Fair enough," Joseph said, his eyes still glued to the wreck of what had been his wife's car.

25

The synagogue office was officially closed on New Year's Eve, but Jeremiah had gone in to do a little catch up work while things were quiet. He knew Cindy was next door at the church taking care of things. Their office was closing at noon. They had plans to meet for a long, leisurely lunch after that. Then in the late afternoon, it was time to start getting ready for the party that night.

Jeremiah was starting to clean up when the door opened. He looked up in surprise as Martin entered the office and made a beeline for him. Martin stopped in front of him and put a large velvet bag on the counter.

"What is that?" Jeremiah asked, eyeing it suspiciously.

"It's a gift for Brenda. It seemed right given what she's gone through. Plus, she lost one of her dollar coins that she's collecting," Martin said with a smile.

"I'm sure she'll be thrilled, but what is in there?"

"A hundred dollar coins, different kinds."

"Wow, that should really make a big impact."

Martin leaned in conspiratorially. "And have her check them closely. I have it on good authority that one of them is worth a lot more than a dollar these days."

"Thank you," Jeremiah said, feeling a surge of emotion. Martin shrugged.

"So, celebrating New Year's with the family?" Jeremiah asked.

Martin nodded. "Got to squeeze in a little more fun before heading back to work."

"Good luck with that," Jeremiah said sincerely.

"Thank you. Happy New Year."

"Same to you."

~

Cindy locked up the office. Fortunately, they were closing early for New Year's Eve. The high schoolers were going to have an all-night party and the church campus would be on lockdown that night. Still, she walked the rounds, making sure that every room they wouldn't be using was sealed up tight.

The sanctuary was unlocked. She opened the door and looked in to see if anyone was still there. Sitting in a pew about halfway toward the front was a lone figure. She walked forward and when she got close she recognized Dave sitting there, staring straight ahead.

It had been a rough year for him with the divorce. She hadn't really had a chance to talk to him since Christmas. She knew he'd been planning to spend it with some cousins.

"Are you okay?" Cindy asked as she sat down next to him in the pew.

"I'm trying to be. And I'm getting there. I've just been talking to God, telling Him that I'm hoping this next year is a better one. I'm looking for peace, and if I can get a little joy, too, it would be great."

She laid a hand on his arm. "I'm sorry."

"Thanks. I'm hoping that Sharna gets a little of those as well. She's a lot worse off than I am."

Cindy frowned. Sharna was the one who had wanted the divorce. For a moment she wondered if the other woman was rethinking her decisions and what that would mean for her and Dave's future.

"She got what she wanted and is regretting it?" Cindy asked.

"I don't know. I think… I think she's ill. I tried to get her the help she needed, but that didn't go well. It's a terrible day when you have to take out a restraining order against someone you love."

Cindy was taken aback. Dave had never said anything about that to her. Somehow, she doubted that he'd told anyone at work.

"What happened?" she asked softly.

"On Mother's Day she showed up at my place. Something had set her off. She came after me with a knife. I think she truly wanted to kill me. Honestly, I'm alive today because of a miracle."

"Dave! I'm so sorry! I had no idea," Cindy said, horrified.

"It's okay, I didn't tell anyone. It's like I didn't want anyone to think less of her, I guess. It was also when I had to face the fact that there really was no way back for us, you know? I mean, I always held out this shred of hope that someday things would be different. That's when I knew that whatever demons she's wrestling with, I can't help her."

"I'm glad you're okay," Cindy said softly.

"Thanks. Me, too. So, here I am, praying and hoping for a better year than this last one."

"I can pray and hope for that for all of us," Cindy said, thinking back on the past year. It had been a rollercoaster.

She'd had some of the greatest moments of her life. She and Jeremiah had become engaged. She'd helped her friend find God. She'd also had some of the worst moments of her life. She'd lost any hope of a relationship with her mother. She still had nightmares about the dark days when Jeremiah had been accused of murder and nearly died. She'd quit her job at the church only to come back.

Dave stood up and she did as well. She walked out of the pew and he followed her. They walked together in silence out of the sanctuary.

"You off to a party?" he asked.

"Yes. Are you going to be okay with the kids?"

"You'll be one of the first to hear if I'm not."

"It's a nice thing you're doing, hosting this sleepover for them."

"It's good for them, good for their parents. And, honestly, I need the distraction tonight," he said with a wan smile.

"Well, have fun."

"I will. Thanks for listening," he said.

"Anytime."

"See you next year," he said with a grin.

"See you next year," she said back.

~

Mark walked into Boone's with Traci, Geanie, Joseph, Cindy and Jeremiah. He wasn't sure what he had expected of a restaurant on top of a fort in a theme park, but it was amazing. Everyone there was dressed to the nines, and he was glad he'd let Traci talk him into wearing a tuxedo.

Josh and Candace saw them and came right over.

"So glad you made it!" Josh said, shaking Mark's hand.

"Thank you for inviting us," Traci said.

"Of course," Candace said cheerfully.

The next four hours he stuffed himself on some of the most amazing food he'd ever had and he even got up and danced on the tiny dance floor three times with Traci. Slowly he could feel all the stress and anxiety of the last few weeks melting away. There was something about the new year that always made even him optimistic about the future. And why shouldn't he be? He had amazing friends, wonderful children, and a beautiful wife who was smiling more tonight than he'd seen her smile in months.

He glanced over toward the dessert table and saw a young woman in a beautiful evening gown hovering near it. There was something in her posture that caught his attention. She was furtive, like she was trying to hide something. Alarm bells went off in his mind, and he started to move closer.

Before he'd made it more than a couple feet she turned around and he realized it was Becca. Her cheeks were puffed out like a chipmunk and she was quickly eating something. From the stain it left on her lips he suspected it was chocolate. Her eyes met his and widened. Very slowly she lifted her hand and placed her finger in front of her lips in a shushing gesture. Clearly, she wanted him to keep this quiet.

He stood there a moment, torn. He'd been told that she had an allergy to sugar which made her a bit crazy. He also knew that she was a grown young woman capable of making her own decisions and it was New Year's Eve. Everyone deserved to let their hair down.

He gave her a brief nod and turned away.

"Everything okay?" Traci asked as he returned his attention to the group.

He smiled at her.

"It is now," he said, giving her a lingering kiss.

When he finally let go of her he looked around at each of his friends. He smiled and nodded at them. They'd been through hell this year and lived to tell about it.

"Here's to a much better year!" he said.

"Here, here," Joseph said enthusiastically.

Geanie and Cindy laughed and nodded. Jeremiah was too busy staring at Cindy with googly eyes to comment. It was going to be a big year for all of them and there was still a lot of wedding planning to do.

"Fifteen minutes left until midnight," Joseph said.

"Watch out, she's loose!" he suddenly heard someone shout across the room.

He turned toward the sound and was shocked to see Becca running while people scattered in front of her. One of them staggered into Mark, sloshing champagne on his shirt.

Becca's hair which had been up in an elegant bun just moments before was now streaming behind her. There was chocolate covering half her face and she was bouncing with each stride.

"What the-"

Three guys, including Josh, descended on her, trying to grab her. She eluded all of them. A big guy that reminded Mark vaguely of a pirate caught her around the middle and lifted her up off her feet. She screeched at the top of her lungs and contorted her body until she could bite his hand. He dropped her with a shout.

She made three enormous jumps, turned and springboarded off the back of some random guy who was down on one knee proposing to his girlfriend.

Becca landed face first on top of the dessert table. Several people surged forward, but then a man's voice rang out loud and clear.

"Stop!"

Mark turned and was stunned to see that it was John Hanson, the owner of The Zone and Josh's father. The former quarterback just shook his head at everyone.

"Tonight our little Becca is here as a guest and what's the first rule of The Zone?" he asked.

The entire crowd responded, "Let players play!"

"Exactly. Everyone deserves one night of celebration. Happy New Year to all!"

Traci burst into genuine laughter, deep and rich and full. It warmed Mark's heart to hear the sound of it and to see the joy on her face in that moment.

"They weren't kidding about her being allergic to sugar," Mark whispered to Joseph, stunned at what he'd just seen.

"I'm glad she wasn't in our house," Joseph said.

Mark looked down at the champagne on his shirt. There was still five minutes left until midnight so he had time to put some water on it.

He excused himself to the restroom. It was down a long corridor which was empty and relatively quiet. His phone rang, and he stopped and pulled it out of his jacket pocket, expecting that it was Liam.

He glanced at the caller id. It read: Unknown. He answered it with a frown.

"Hello?"

"Hello, Detective," a deep male voice said. "I just wanted to wish you a happy New Year."

Mark didn't know why, but something about the voice sent a shiver up his spine. His first instinct was to hang up, but he forced himself to stay on the call.

"Who is this?" he asked, struggling to keep his voice even and not betray the deep sense of fear he was feeling.

"I'm sorry, Mark, I forgot that we haven't yet been properly introduced. My voice is unfamiliar to you even though I have heard yours many, many times. By the way, give my love to Traci. Such a sweet woman. I was sorry to hear that she's having a bit of a, how should I call it, a nervous breakdown. One can't blame her, really. Not with all she's been through."

"You leave my wife alone!" Mark hissed.

"I assure you I have no intention of harming her…for now."

"What do you want and who are you?" Mark demanded.

From the main room of the restaurant he heard someone shout, "Five minutes until midnight!"

"Honestly, I'm surprised you haven't guessed the latter. I thought you were brighter than that. Maybe there's a reason my son never trusted you with his secrets."

"Your son? Who's your-"

Mark stopped speaking as the terrible truth hit him. He was speaking to Not Paul's father.

Matthews chuckled. "I think you finally figured out the 'who'. Now for the 'what'. I'm just calling to extend holiday greetings to you, as I said before. I also wanted to say one more thing."

"What's that?" Mark whispered.

"See you next year."

The Zone referees in this book are from the Sweet Seasons series.

Follow the adventures of Candace, Josh, Becca, and the others in:

The Summer of Cotton Candy
The Fall of Candy Corn
The Winter of Candy Canes
The Spring of Candy Apples
The Summer of Rice Candy
The Fall of Candy Bars (coming 2020)

And see the Psalm 23 Mysteries characters co-star in:

The Winter of Candy Kisses (coming 2020)

~

Love the Psalm 23 Mysteries? Check out Debbie Viguié's newest mystery series: **A Salty Tale Mystery**.

The Spice of Life
Book 2 (coming 2020)

Read the first chapter of *The Spice of Life* in the next pages!

1

Everyone thought that Anise Salis had killed her husband, Frank. Mornings like this she wished that she had. It was six in the morning and she was staring down a long day taking inventory of her spice shop by herself. She hated the biannual ritual but it was unfortunately a necessary evil. For the occasion she had pulled her shoulder-length auburn hair into a lopsided bun on top of her head. It wasn't high fashion, but no one had ever accused her of caring much for her appearance anyway. When she had turned thirty a few grey hairs had appeared as if by magic. She'd been debating whether or not to do anything about them. Five years later she still hadn't made up her mind.

She'd been planning on grabbing a bagel on her way into the shop, but her stomach was growling, and she really didn't want to get started. Anise made a quick decision and veered into Aunties, an old-fashioned style diner that was practically an institution in the small New England town of Port James.

Anise sat down at the counter inside. Three seats down from her was a man in a worn army jacket with long, shaggy dark hair. He looked to be in his early thirties. He was clutching a cup of coffee in both hands, his long fingers flexing and relaxing in rapid cycles on the ceramic. He was cleanshaven and Anise noticed that he had a handsome face despite the fact that his cheeks were gaunt and he looked like it had been a long time since he'd had regular meals.

She turned away as the waitress, Peggy, came over.

"The usual?" Peggy asked without preamble.

"Yeah," Anise said.

Peggy didn't like her. She did like gossiping about her, though. Peggy was one of the central hubs of information in Port James. At least her personal dislike didn't get in the way of her getting Anise her food fast. She always suspected, though, that the other woman was in a hurry to get rid of her.

A couple minutes later Anise was busy eating an omelet while watching Peggy size up the stranger. Peggy refilled the man's coffee cup which was still pretty full.

"So, stranger, what's your name?" Peggy asked.

"Mine?" he asked, staring at her.

"I don't see any other strangers here," Peggy said, her fake smile cracking slightly.

"Um, Lincoln," he said.

"So, Lincoln, are you going to order some food or just sit here staring at your coffee?" Peggy asked.

Anise winced. Peggy wasn't always the nicest or the most subtle person on the planet.

"Just…coffee," Lincoln said slowly.

He can't afford food, she realized. Before she knew what she was doing, Anise pulled a ten-dollar bill out of her purse and put it on the counter. "Breakfast is on me."

Lincoln turned and looked at her then. His eyes were a piercing blue but there was something dark in them, something haunted. She felt the hair stand up on the back of her neck as he scowled at her.

"I don't take charity," he said gruffly. "I work for what's mine."

He kept Anise pinned with his stare as she slowly put the money back in her purse. There was something dangerous about him. Dangerous and broken. Her father used to tell her about guys like him that he occasionally came across in his work with veterans.

"Where do you work?" Peggy pressed.

Lincoln turned back to her and Anise felt a sense of relief when his eyes were no longer burning through her.

"Nowhere at the moment. Know anyone looking for help?"

"Not around here," Peggy said emphatically. It was clear she didn't like him.

Peggy put the handwritten check for Anise's breakfast down next to her while still keeping her eyes glued on Lincoln. Anise finished up the last couple bites of her omelet then paid. She was at the door when she found herself turning around.

"You ever do store inventory?" she asked before she could stop herself.

Lincoln turned and looked at her. "Once or twice," he said slowly.

"I own a spice shop and I have to do inventory. I'll pay you one hundred dollars if we get it all done today," she said.

Lincoln nodded. "Let me finish my coffee."

"I'll wait outside," Anise said, walking out.

She couldn't believe she had done that. The help would be fantastic, but she didn't normally like people. Then again, most people had never given her any reason to. There was something about him, though. Maybe it was just that Peggy seemed to dislike him even more than she did Anise.

Lincoln was out a minute later. He was tall, well over six feet and she had to crane her neck a bit to look up at him.

"Lincoln," he said, offering her his hand.

She shook it. "Anise."

"How do you spell that?"

"A-N-I-S-E," she said. It wasn't the first time someone had asked.

"Same spelling as the spice?"

"Yes," she said, struggling to hide her surprise.

"And you have a spice shop?"

"Yup. Speaking of, it's this way," she said, starting to walk down the street.

He walked beside her and she couldn't help but notice that he moved with a sort of raw power and strength. Like in the coffee shop, though, he fidgeted with his hands, clenching and unclenching his fingers.

"It's a block from the water," she said, feeling the silence pressing in on her. Normally she preferred silence, but the whole situation was unfamiliar, and it was making her a bit uncomfortable.

"Salt store near the salt water?"

"It's more than just salt. But, yes, the irony is not lost on me," she said.

The truth was none of that had been her choice. It had been her husband's. Since he'd run off she'd been stuck with it and so many other of his life choices.

"You don't like salt?"

"No, I do, it's just… complicated," she said.

The store was on the corner of an old brick building and actually faced toward the ocean. When they reached the block it was on she began to walk faster and Lincoln kept pace. As they neared the corner she noticed glass glittering on the sidewalk. Someone must have had an accident and lost a windshield. There were no windows on that side of her store so it couldn't be from that.

They rounded the corner and Anise lunged forward with a gasp. The front door of her shop was hanging wide open, nearly ripped from its hinges. The glass from the front door was everywhere. She made it to the door, glanced inside and screamed. A man was lying face down in a pool of blood just inside the door.

There was a lot of blood. Lincoln could smell it. It wasn't fresh, it had been there a couple of hours. The woman was screaming in his ear and it hurt his head. He wanted to tell her to stop but that might be rude. She had offered to pay him after all.

"Maybe you should call someone," he said slowly.

She turned and looked at him.

"I don't want to," he said. "I don't like phones."

She thought he was crazy. He could tell. That was okay. He was used to it. It was easier that way. People left crazy people alone and that was just fine with him. When people got close they wanted to talk, to understand. They wanted answers. And he had none he could give. No easy ones at any rate.

She pulled a phone out of her purse and a moment later had called 911. She was upset, but at least she had stopped screaming. He stared at the body while she talked to the dispatcher.

The dead man was a couple inches short of six feet with light brown hair. He had broad shoulders, large hands, and was carrying at least ten extra pounds on him. He was dressed all in black, perfect for breaking in someplace.

Anise finally ended her call. "Who is he?" she asked, her voice shaking slightly.

The man was facedown so unless she recognized something about his build there was no telling if she knew the man until they could actually make out his features. She wanted an answer now.

"Possibly ex-military," Lincoln said. It wasn't much but it was all he could offer her.

"How do you know?"

"His boots."

He looked past the dead man into the interior of the shop. Shelves lined the walls all around with rows and rows of spice jars visible. Everything was neat except for one spot in the back where a two-and-a-half foot wide section of shelves was barren, its contents dumped all over the floor in haphazard fashion. Many of the containers had broken and there was a rainbow of colors swirling around the floor. The red could be cinnamon or it could be alaea salt from Hawaii which got its color from red volcanic clay.

"Is that a salt section or a spice section?" he asked Anise.

"What?"

"The wall where all the spices have been dumped on the floor. What section was it?"

"Um, I don't know."

254

"It's your store. Why don't you know?" he asked.

"Maybe because there's a dead body in the doorway and I can't think straight!" she shouted at him.

He turned and looked at Anise. Her skin was flushed, her pupils dilated, and she was shaking slightly. She was going into shock.

"That seems fair," he said.

He shrugged out of his jacket and handed it to her. "Put this on. It will keep you warmer while you're in shock."

He expected her to refuse. It was a sorry looking jacket offered to her by a stranger whom she had no reason to trust. To his surprise she took it with a muttered "thank you" and slipped it on. She looked tiny inside it, lost. He felt that way a lot. He also felt cold all the time, but on the inside, and no matter how hot it was outside the jacket never helped. Nothing ever helped.

In the distance he could hear sirens and he flinched. He didn't like loud noises, the kind that hurt the ears and pierced the heart. He stood his ground, though, waiting.

"They're almost here," he told Anise, mostly just to say something. If he was talking he wasn't as inside his own head as he was if he was just quiet and thinking.

"Okay," she said.

He could tell she wasn't even hearing the sirens. Her gaze was riveted on the dead man. She was in shock and she was horrified but it didn't look like she was going to throw up. He respected her for that. A lot of people did, especially the first or second time.

"You're going to be okay," he said.

That got through to her and she turned and looked at him. "I wasn't thinking about me," she said. "I was wondering who he is, if he has family, who did this to him."

She rose even more in his estimation. Before he could say anything else an ambulance came into view being chased by two cop cars. They all came to an abrupt stop just a few feet away and people poured out of them. The first to reach them were the EMTs, one of whom gently moved Anise to the side where she wasn't in the way. The man maneuvered her in such a way that she could no longer see the body. It was smart.

Lincoln thought about leaving. There were people here now to take care of her and this wasn't any of his affair. Best not to get involved. She had his jacket, though, and she had offered him work in the shop today and he had agreed. It wouldn't be honorable to just take off even if the nature of the work was suddenly very much changed.

A man with a sheriff's badge approached them while two other police officers went inside with the EMTs. He had gray hair and a jutting jaw, a hard jaw. He had hard eyes to go with it. Lincoln clenched his fists and gritted his teeth.

"Anise, what happened here?" the man boomed.

"I was coming to work and I found all that," she said waving her hand toward the door.

"Did you go inside?"

"No, Bill, I called 911 straight away."

Lincoln noted the use of the sheriff's first name. She knew the man. Then again it was a small town, he probably shouldn't be too surprised. Bill's eyes shifted to him.

"And who is this?"

"Lincoln," he said quietly.

"I hired him to help me take inventory today," Anise said.

"So, you know this guy?" Bill said, eyes taking him in. Lincoln could tell the sheriff also took note of the fact that Anise was wearing his jacket.

"We just met this morning at the diner," Lincoln said. He didn't want the man making any assumptions about their relationship. For either of their sakes.

"Peggy was there," Anise said quickly.

Lincoln glanced at her. Clearly she didn't trust the sheriff to just take her word on things if she was calling in a witness so quickly.

"Sheriff?" one of the deputies said, voice strained as he stepped out of the store.

"What is it, Jeffrey?"

"Deputy Hudson."

"What about him? He call in finally?"

"No, sir. The body. It's Deputy Hudson."

The sheriff turned red and jabbed his finger at Anise. "I told him if he poked around here long enough there'd be trouble."

Lincoln didn't like the aggressive stance the man was taking with Anise. She was trying to shy away from him, but her back was already against the brick wall and there was nowhere to go.

"Maybe give the lady a little space," he said, knowing he shouldn't get involved. It was stupid to antagonize local law enforcement. It never ended well.

"This ain't no lady, son. You're going to want to get away from her right now."

"Why?" Lincoln asked, because apparently he was just too stupid or stubborn to do as the man said.

"She's a murderer. She killed her husband and now she's killed that man in there."

Debbie Viguié is the New York Times Bestselling author of more than two dozen novels including the *Wicked* series, the *Crusade* series and the *Wolf Springs Chronicles* series co-authored with Nancy Holder. Debbie also writes thrillers including *The Psalm 23 Mysteries,* the *Kiss* trilogy, and the *Witch Hunt* trilogy. When Debbie isn't busy writing she enjoys spending time with her husband, Scott, visiting theme parks. They live in Florida with their cat, Schrödinger.

CPSIA information can be obtained
at www.ICGtesting.com
Printed in the USA
LVHW021655150621
690286LV00006B/960

9 781733 428125